TAZHIO

KIRENAI FATED MATES

TAMSIN LEY

Twin Leaf Press

All characters in this book, be they supernatural, human, or something else entirely, are the product of the author's imagination. Any resemblance to actual people, situations, or events are entirely coincidental.

Cover by The Book Brander

Paperback version
ISBN-13: 978-1-950027-99-6
Copyright © 2022 Twin Leaf Press
All rights reserved.

Twin Leaf Press
PO Box 672255
Chugiak, AK 99567

Tazhio

As a shuttle pilot on board the starship *Romantasy*, I'm not supposed to get involved with the passengers. Yet the moment I meet the timid human female with the stowaway quadruped, I can't get her out of my mind. And avoiding her isn't an option...

Tamara

I hate to travel. Loathe it, in fact. I'm quite happy sitting at home with my dog and making custom embroidery to sell on Etsy. But when I win tickets to an intergalactic singles cruise, my sisters bully me into going. The next thing I know, I'm acting stupid over a shuttle pilot with brilliant blue skin and a smile that could melt the clothes right off my body.

Then a freak accident strands us on a hostile alien planet and not only does it look like I'll never see home again, but the locals are hell-bent on rutting with anything female. The only way to stop them is to let Tazhio claim me. And once he claims me, I'll belong to him forever...

Dear reader,

Be sure to check out the glossary at the bac[k]
are into that sort of thing. Plus there is a
section with descriptions of the alien races y[ou]
encounter in this series. Happy reading!

Tamsin

TAMARA

*D*o *aliens ever get motion sick?* I can't stop the thought rolling around in my head as our limo turns down the palm-tree-lined street leading to the spaceport. My stomach roils, despite the prescription patch my sister, Suzanne, affixed behind my ear. I got through a commercial flight and a car ride, but I dread boarding the space shuttle that will transport us to the cruise ship waiting in orbit.

I stare out the window and chew my nail, my other hand clutched in Beanie's fur. My six-pound chihuahua is laid back, as usual, a ball of heat on my lap. My sisters tried to talk me out of bringing him along, but this entire escapade is so far outside my comfort zone, I'm worried even he won't provide enough emotional support. *Why did I let them talk me into this?*

Suzanne grabs my wrist, pulling my hand away from my mouth. Her red-gold hair falls in a perfect swish over her forehead, and her green eyes are compassionate. "Stop it, Tamara. You're going to ruin your manicure."

I curl my fingers into my palm to hide the chipped red paint. I'm not really a mani-pedi kind of person, but my sisters insisted I had to dress up to travel first class. After several hours of travel, I'm feeling anything but classy. And we haven't even made it into space yet. My green peekaboo blouse keeps slipping off my shoulders, and the stretchy waistband has rolled uncomfortably down under my belly. I wish I'd put my foot down about the clothes. Or put my foot down about this entire trip.

But I've never been good at standing up for myself.

All three of my sisters chatter excitedly about their upcoming plans, but I'm barely listening until my twin sister, Jennifer, nudges my knee. "I said, let me see your phone."

She's sitting across from us with her back to the driver. The enormous case containing her astronomy equipment rests on the seat beside her. She's dreamed of going to space since we were kids, and is the main reason I couldn't say no to the trip.

"Why do you want our phones?" Our younger sister, Bethany, clutches the sparkly case of her phone against her chest. As usual, she looks stunning in her flouncy yellow sundress, her wavy auburn hair freshly cut and styled. Our little sister is outgoing, loud, and always looks like she's about ready to go on TV—which makes sense because she hosts a popular television cooking show.

Jennifer wrestles Bethany's phone out of her grip. "I'm installing an app that will let us document any spatial events or anomalies."

I hand my phone over without a word. I know better than to argue.

"I'm not going on this cruise to spend my time gathering data for you." Suzanne tries to snatch her phone back, but Jennifer bats her hand away. "The only research I want to do is which alien has the tightest abs."

"Chill," Jennifer says. "I'm amping up our Bluetooth signals so the phones will stay tethered, even without cell service. That way, we can keep track of each other while we're fending off horny aliens."

"God, I hope they're horny." Suzanne sighs. "I've swiped nothing but duds on Bumble lately." Newly divorced with both kids off to college, Suzanne's a free agent for the first time in nineteen years. Another reason I can't say no to this trip.

I, on the other hand, have zero desire to meet eligible men, let alone alien men, not with my track record. My last boyfriend gave me the "it's not you, it's me" speech, then promptly moved in with another woman. Other than the mandatory parties we're to attend, I plan on holing up in my room with Beanie and my latest embroidery project.

Bethany leans over my lap to peer out the tinted window. "I see the shuttle!"

"Whoa." Suzanne crowds in, her elbow pressing me back against the seat. "Those are aliens!"

I squirm and shove her off me, feeling nauseous. "You're making me sick."

"Really, Tamara?" Bethany backs off. "Are you ever going to let that go? It was a million years ago."

Suzanne pushes aside my hair to check behind my ear. "Is the patch not working?"

"Stop." I shrug her hand away. "I just need space."

Memories of my tenth-grade trip to Europe still haunt me. I'd embarrassed myself by barfing all over the flight attendant's shoes. Afterward, the other kids ridiculed me mercilessly, and for the rest of high school I was called the vomit queen.

I roll down the window, and muggy air that smells like hot pavement blasts me in the face. Ahead on the tarmac, I see something that looks like an enormous purple rosebud resting on its side. My throat tightens.

One side of the ship is rolled open to form a ramp, and three broad-shouldered men wearing white uniforms wait at the base. Their skin is blue, just like in the Hallmark movies. It seems like every television show has featured a blue alien hero since an alien prince came to Earth looking for a mate last year.

The limo rolls to a stop about thirty feet from the ramp. Before the driver can get out to open our door, Suzanne flings it open and clambers out with

Bethany right on her heels. Jennifer opens the door on our side, tugging her case from the seat.

I take my time gathering Beanie back into my purse and putting on my sunglasses. I can't believe I'm doing this. Teeth clenched, I step out of the limo onto the tarmac, heat permeating the thin soles of my sandals. My mouth goes dry as I look up at the big alien ship. The lavender surface sparkles slightly in the sunlight and has ribbed veins like an actual rose petal. *How can this possibly be strong enough to go into space?*

Suzanne is already strolling up the ramp, grinning like a Cheshire cat and chatting with an alien carrying two of their over-sized suitcases. Another alien has hoisted Jennifer's enormous astronomy case from the car while Jennifer flutters around like a worried mother hen. I'm struck by how similar all the blue guys seem to appear, a bit like blue Ken dolls in matching white uniforms.

Bethany looks toward me, eyes hidden behind gold-mirrored designer shades. "Ready?"

I nod but remain rooted in place as my sister strolls toward the ramp without me.

The limo pulls away, too, leaving me standing sentinel on the tarmac with the sun beating down on my head. Sweat rolls down my cleavage and sticks my shirt against my back. Beanie is probably cooking alive in my purse. Swallowing my impending terror, I move toward the waiting ramp.

A baffle wall just inside the open hatch blocks my view of the shuttle's interior, but I can hear cheerful chatter from inside. My sisters are too excited to notice I'm missing. *If I don't get on, will the shuttle leave without me?*

I pivot, taking a wistful look at the hangars surrounding the airfield. I see a couple of guys standing in the shade against one wall, smoking. Even though I don't smoke, I'm tempted to go ask them for a puff, just for an excuse to delay boarding.

"Are you ready?"

I jump at the sudden deep voice, catching my purse before it slips completely off my shoulder. Poor Beanie whines as he's jostled inside. A tall blue man in a white uniform stands on the shuttle ramp watching me intently. He looks less human than the ones who helped my sisters, with eyes that are slightly too big for his chiseled face, but he's dressed in the same white one-piece uniform. His deep blue hair is lustrous and thick, shorter along the sides and curling against his collar in the back.

His gaze lowers to my purse, and nervous guilt rocks through me. The cruise line hadn't asked about paperwork for Beanie, and I figured it was better to ask forgiveness than permission, especially since some facilities don't consider emotional support dogs true service animals. Now all I can think is that my sisters will kill me if Beanie gets us banned from the trip.

The alien steps forward and reaches for my purse. "Allow me to assist."

I adjust my purse under my arm protectively, and Beanie whines again. The alien frowns and draws his hand back.

"It's a service animal," I assure him. "He doesn't bite, I promise."

The alien moves sideways, keeping his gaze on my bag. His muscles are quite evident under his uniform, and I can't help wondering if he looks human under his clothes. I bite my lip, my heart beating faster as he shifts his gaze back to mine. The moment his midnight blue eyes meet mine, I'm swept by a moment of vertigo, and my thundering heart goes into overdrive. *Holy shit, the TV shows didn't do their alien heroes justice.* To be fair, the shows only had access to human actors painted blue, but damn, if a real Kirenai ever took to the screen, he'd be an immediate superstar. I've never felt this kind of attraction to a man in my life, let alone one I just met.

"The pattern is a remarkable likeness." His voice feels like heavy silk settling over my skin.

I blink dumbly at him a moment, trying to make sense of his comment. "Um, what?"

He gestures toward my purse. "I've never seen this type of artwork before."

I look down at it, realizing he must mean the embroidered image of Beanie. "Oh! Thank you. I sell custom embroidery on Etsy."

"You made it?"

"Yes." I automatically fumble inside the bag for one of my cards and hold it out. "If you're interested, let me know. I can work from a picture."

He glances down without taking it. "Perhaps another time." He gestures toward the hatch. "We are running behind schedule. Please follow me."

Disappointment floods me as he strides up the ramp without looking back, and I kick myself. *He was just being polite.* No way a hot guy like him is interested—not in me or my embroidery. At least he didn't kick me off the trip because of Beanie.

I hurry up the ramp, towing my suitcase behind me. Inside the shuttle, the alien ducks through a round doorway which immediately spirals closed behind him. In the other direction, the passenger area is lined with plush red chairs, some obviously not proportioned for humans.

One of the blue alien stewards urges me down the aisle. "This way, miss. May I take your suitcase? We're about to take off."

I gulp, suddenly realizing who I was talking to down on the tarmac. *The pilot.* The pilot himself came to make certain I got on board. Now I feel like everyone is looking at me, judging me for making them late. *Great start to the trip.* I relinquish the handle of my suitcase, spotting Suzanne and Bethany sitting next to each other near a window.

Jennifer is hovering behind the porter who's manhandling her massive telescope case down the aisle at the back.

A whooshing sound heralds what I assume must be the ramp furling closed, and the floor begins to vibrate softly. My stomach lurches, and I flail one hand to support myself against the nearby wall, fighting back the vivid memory of my tenth-grade trip. *Do not vomit.*

The steward puts a hand to my elbow. "Are you all right, miss?"

Afraid to open my mouth, I nod fiercely and plop down in the nearest seat. The sunlight streaming through the window slices across my face as the shuttle pivots. *We're moving.* Terror grips my heart, and I search for a seatbelt. There are none. Don't these aliens have safety protocols? I squeeze my eyes shut, breathing slowly through my nose.

Beanie wriggles free of the bag, settling on my lap. I stroke his shoulders and rump, not sure if he's calming me or the other way around at this point.

Someone takes a seat next to me, and I crack one eye to see Jennifer looking at me with a raised eyebrow. "Patch still not working?"

I make a sour face. "I'm super sensitive, all right?"

Jennifer sighs. "Okay, sorry. But if you're going to sit there with your eyes closed, can I at least have the window seat?"

Clenching my teeth, I push to my feet and let her swap. "I hope you know how much you owe me for all this."

"I know, I know. Thanks." Jennifer turns and presses her face to the window.

I sit stiffly in the other seat and squeeze my eyes shut, forcing myself to keep my touch gentle as I pet Beanie's back. If I manage to finish this cruise without embarrassing myself again, it will be a miracle.

2

TAZHIO

*T*he copper-haired female feels like it's put my compass off balance. I stare at the flight controls, feeling like I'm stuck in a tailspin. *Pull yourself together.*

It seems that the rumors about human females are true, and I want her, bad. But the crew has been instructed not to involve themselves with the humans. The Intergalactic Dating Agency takes pride in its success rate and screens guests to ensure there is at least one genetically viable match on board for each paying guest—not shuttle pilots like me.

I fire up the engines and focus on getting us free of the planet's gravitational pull. Soon the joy of flying once more captures my attention, and I take us on a full turn around the *Romantasy* to give the passengers a view of the cruise ship before they board. The habitat ring reflects the golden light from this solar system's intense sun, and I'm tempted to make a flyby of the control module in the center just for fun. But we've fallen behind schedule, so I resist and deposit this batch of passengers before heading back to Earth for the next round.

All day long, I stay in the cockpit and let the stewards and porters handle the incoming females. I can't risk being distracted again. But it seems it's too late for that. I keep picturing the copper-haired female's pale freckled cheeks and gray eyes, the way her blouse hugged her curves in all the right places. She seemed hesitant, furtive, and guilty—not usually the qualities I look for in a female companion. Yet the tangle of feelings roiling in my chest feels like navigating a spatial anomaly without a map.

After I'm done shuttling passengers, I return to my quarters and look up her picture on the shuttle manifest. I know I shouldn't, but I can't stop myself. Her name is Tamara Bloom. She's here with three siblings—imagine having three! Her cabin is on the third tier, inner ring. *I'll need to avoid that area of the ship.* Not that I have reason to go strolling through the passenger decks.

Yet my legs are aching to go for a walk down that corridor at this very moment.

Trying to focus on anything but her, I begin a post-check of the shuttle's comm array. Shuttle maintenance isn't my favorite thing—I much prefer flying, but I need something to do. Across the bay, several mechanics crack dirty jokes about lubing hydraulics. The sex talk turns my mind back to Tamara.

What the kuzara *is wrong with me?* I met the human once, and briefly, yet the moment our eyes connected, my matrix sparked with desire. *The last thing I need is a female distracting me from my job.*

I'm staring sightlessly at a receptor panel embedded in the hull with a spanner clutched uselessly in one hand when a familiar voice calls my name. "Tazhio, you ready?"

I look up and spot a Kirenai heading my direction across the shuttle bay floor. *Kiozhi?* He's shaped like a human wearing black-and-white Earth clothing.

Unlike me, Kiozhi is a guest on the *Romantasy*. He's one of the most eligible bachelors in the galaxy and a longtime family friend. But he's as comfortable among the mechanics as he is with his billionaire buddies, and he side-steps a mechanized cart trundling across the deck before coming to a stop beside me. He frowns at the tool in my hands. "What are you doing down here? The party's already thumping up on the observation deck, and you promised to be my 'wing-friend,' remember?"

"I think you mean wingman," I correct the human term. I only remember it because it refers to flying.

"Oh, right." He smooths the lapels of his suit jacket. "I'm glad you remember this stuff, Tazhio. Let's get going."

The last thing I want to do is go mill around a hundred human women who might drive me out of my mind. "Sorry, I can't make it. I need to make sure this shuttle is ready for tomorrow's excursion."

"Isn't that their job?" Kiozhi motions toward the mechanics. "You promised you'd have my back. The females are accustomed to males with wingmen, and I plan to be exactly what they desire."

I shake my head and smirk, thinking of the scores of women I've seen on my friend's arm. "I don't think you'll have any trouble getting a female without me."

Kiozhi scowls. "Tonight is different. I'm supposed to have an actual, viable match right here on this ship. You have to come with me and keep me on track so I can find her. You owe me that much."

"*Kuzara*," I swear. I do owe my friend for bailing out my family's art gallery during the last recession. "Fine. But after tonight, we're even, okay?"

"Sure we are." Grinning, Kiozhi leads the way to the maintenance lift.

Crew members aren't invited to social events, but Kiozhi is rich enough to get what he wants, and he wants me there. I change into a fresh uniform, and a few minutes later, we're standing shoulder-to-shoulder among hundreds of people on the *Romantasy's* vast observation deck. A nebula is visible through the translucent ceiling, bathing guests in a shifting rainbow of light. From the stage in the center, a band plays an upbeat tune, and the floor teems with human females in all manner of dresses, from short and slinky to long and elegant.

The air smells of lust and perfume, and I can't help myself—I scan the room for a tantalizing glint of copper-colored hair. Quite a few women have varying shades of red, auburn, or even fuchsia hair, but I can't spot Tamara among the sea of unfamiliar faces.

"Come on." Kiozhi elbows me and presses into the crowd.

I follow, my *Iki'i* thrumming with the anticipation and excitement filling the room. I'm relieved to discover that none of the females seem to affect me as Tamara did, and I pass them by politely. Perhaps what I experienced earlier was a fluke, a residual effect of my excitement to be flying around a new planet. I'd been horny after an exhilarating flight before.

Kiozhi pauses next to a group of females and introduces himself, striking up an easy conversation. I have zero interest in these females, so I nod politely, half-listening as I look around.

A passing tray of *sowain* nuggets catches my attention, and I snag a morsel, popping it in my mouth and chewing slowly. The chefs have outdone themselves, and delicacies from around the galaxy are lavishly displayed on long tables around the room. I grab a tall, thin glass of *Lensoran* bubbly and take a sip.

Red hair near the kitchen doors catches my attention, but it's only a small congregation of Fogarians, their classic russet skin and thick bodies shorter than most of the females. Most of the guests cluster in species-specific groupings. Besides the human females, there are pale Vatosangans, diminutive Hage, and even one Klen, his long green eyestalks drawn close to his skull as if attempting to make his broad-mouthed face look more human. I can't help chuckling when I notice a pair of females gawking at a stone-skinned Khargal who is smugly flexing his admittedly impressive wings. The humans are obviously trying to be subtle, but failing miserably.

Then I spot a flash of copper, and it's as if my shuttle's view screen has suddenly zoomed in on a target. *Tamara*. She stands near the far wall in a sleeveless, emerald-green dress that exposes her pale, freckled shoulders and hugs the delicious curves of her breasts before flaring into ruffled tiers to her knees. She's smiling at a Fogarian with spiked crimson hair and shaggy sideburns.

My insides tense and I clench my jaw. My mind is irrationally demanding, *mine*. I take another sip of my bubbly, trying to calm my senses. What is the Fogarian saying to her? Tamara's smile is cordial, but even with her out of range of my *Iki'i*, I can tell she's feeling uncomfortable. There's a tightness to her eyes, a stiffness to her posture.

A blue hand waves in front of my face. "Hey, you okay?"

I blink at Kiozhi and nod. "Yeah. You're doing great."

"What are you talking about?" My friend's upper lip curls in frustration. "Those females just giggled and walked away. I wonder if I should take off my shirt like those Kirenai over there."

I don't bother looking where Kiozhi's pointing. I can't take my eyes off Tamara. She shifts her large purse to her opposite shoulder, away from the Fogarian, and her smile is now gone. She's shaking her head.

Suddenly, I recall her purse. She had a creature inside—a symbiote, I assume. I meant to ask the steward on the shuttle to document it, but I was so wrapped up in avoiding the females, I forgot. Which means that technically, the creature can be considered vermin and fair game for the Fogarian or any of the other races who enjoy hunting their meals.

Kuzara. If anything happens to her companion, it will be my fault. Before I realize what I'm doing, I push through the crowd toward her. I hear Kiozhi call my name, but don't stop.

"Excuse me?" A female with golden brown hair and enormous silver hoop earrings steps into my path. "You were our shuttle pilot, right?"

I smile politely and try to edge sideways around her. "Yes."

The female puts a hand on my forearm and raises her voice toward a nearby group of her companions. "I told you!" Turning back to face me, she says, "My friends and I are having trouble telling ya'll apart. But I'd recognize those big blue eyes of yours anywhere."

For the first time, I wonder if choosing not to adopt a basic human structure like the other Kirenai crew members might be a mistake. I say, "Many humans look the same to us as well."

"Well, I would love to get to know you better." Hand still gripping my arm, she gestures to a group of human females on the dance floor near the stage, spinning and twirling. "Ever dance with a human before?"

Kiozhi pulls to a stop beside me, radiating frustration. "Where are you going in such a hurry?" Then he seems to notice the female. "Well, hello."

Thank the gods. I move the female's hand from my arm to his. "Kiozhi, this lady would like to dance."

Without waiting to see how that will go over, I resume course.

Except the landmarks have shifted, and she's no longer in the same place.

Concern rising, I pull my matrix into a taller shape, ignoring the gasps of shock from the nearby humans. Scanning the crowd over everyone's head, I spot Tamara and the Fogarian moving toward the dance floor. He's all but dragging her, his meaty hand clamped tightly around her wrist.

Mine. Baring my teeth, I cut through the crowd toward them.

3

TAMARA

I feel like I've been conned into a timeshare presentation that will last two weeks instead of two hours. Is every mandatory party going to be like this? The rotund alien with crimson hair and sideburns refuses to take no for an answer, and now he's insisting I dance with him. Or *for* him, I'm not sure. All I know is that his clawed grip feels like a vise around my wrist as he drags me forward.

"Thank you, but really, I don't dance," I say. The thought of flailing around in front of all these people makes my heartbeat feel like an earthquake inside my chest.

"I'm going to teach you the Fogarian waltz," the alien shouts over his shoulder as he zig-zags behind a group of gray aliens with wings.

Hoping for an out, I search the crowd for one of my sisters. Suzanne has her back to me and is happily chatting with a group of blue aliens, looking glamorous in her bright red cocktail dress. Jennifer, dressed in a simple black sheath dress, is staring at her phone and ignoring two blue aliens trying to catch her attention. And Bethany is nowhere in sight, probably in the kitchens chatting to someone about the food.

I try jerking my hand free and accidentally elbow a woman in the boob. I cringe-smile at her. "I'm so sorry!"

The woman, wearing a black silk gown slit to expose one shapely leg, levels a haughty glare at me, then sweeps her gaze over the tight bodice of my borrowed dress. With a sniff, she turns away. The dress is Jennifer's, and I wore it because my sisters insisted I looked good in it. Big fat liars. I knew it showed too much cleavage. *This is why I prefer to stay home.*

The last thing I want to do is join the graceful couples twirling around the glossy dance floor as if they've taken dance lessons their entire lives. Everyone at the party tonight is glamorous, all glitter and silk.

"Please, I'm not a dancer," I beg again, hoping he'll listen.

"It isn't difficult, I promise," he shouts without looking back.

Beanie whines softly, conscious of my distress. I cling to my purse strap with my free hand, fighting to keep it up on my shoulder as I'm jostled by the crowd. Suzanne tried to convince me to leave Beanie in my cabin, but a party is exactly the place I need him most. I yearn to go back to my room and hide.

Suddenly, a large blue hand clamps down on the clawed alien's wrist, stopping us in our tracks. "The lady doesn't wish to dance with you."

The deep voice is familiar, and I let my gaze travel from the blue hand up the white uniform sleeve to a broad shoulder. I suck in a breath at the sight of a handsome blue face with large, dark eyes.

Tazhio. I remember hearing this voice over the speaker on the shuttle when our pilot introduced himself. He's even more attractive than I remember. Unlike the other blue aliens who reminded me of Ken dolls with similar short haircuts, tall, muscular bodies, and gleaming smiles, Tazhio is unique. His hair is cut longer, and his square jaw and masculine nose are unmistakable.

Realizing my mouth's hanging open, I snap it closed.

The squat alien releases my hand and shakes himself free from Tazhio's grasp. His hairy face scrunches into a scowl so deep, his eyebrows nearly meet his mustache. "She has not expressed aversion to my invitation."

Tazhio cuts a glance toward me. "Do you wish to accompany this man?"

Cringing at being put on the spot, I shake my head no and quickly shove my newly freed hand inside my bag to touch Beanie's comforting warmth. A warm wet tongue bathes my knuckles, but his kisses can't stop my trembling.

With an indignant huff, the red alien pivots and stalks away.

The relief that floods me feels like a shot of good alcohol, leaving me weak in the knees. I smile at Tazhio. "Thank you."

He puts a hand to the small of my back—an intimate gesture that sends a giddy thrill into my pelvis. It's been a long, long time since I felt anything like that, and without thinking, I take a small step closer. "My name's Tamara."

"Hello, Tamara. I'm Tazhio." He continues gazing at me with an expression that makes my heart flutter. "I suggest you be more assertive about what you want. Would you like an escort back to your cabin?"

I'm not sure how long I'm required to stay to fulfill the requirement for our free tickets, but Tazhio is part of the crew, so if he says I can go, I'll take it. "If that would be all right, yes."

Hand still on my back, he guides me toward the lift platform, joining two other couples. One pair is making out like teenagers and the other is exchanging glances that drip with lust. Embarrassed and slightly aroused, I keep my gaze on the floor as the lift descends. The lust-filled couple exits first, then the kissers. Now alone in the lift with Tazhio, I look up to find him staring at me.

Whoa, Nelly. There can be no mistaking the desire in his eyes.

My heart rises into my throat and my nipples get all prickly feeling inside my too-tight bodice. I hadn't had a partner that didn't require batteries since my last boyfriend left me two years ago, and the idea of Tazhio's hands on me is irresistible. *Should I invite him for a nightcap?* This is a singles cruise, after all, and Suzanne had insisted on stashing a pack of condoms in my room "just in case."

Before I can second-guess myself, I reach over and twine my fingers with his, trying to smile in invitation.

His weight shifts away from me, and a lump fills my throat. My fingers turn icy. *Shit.* I misread him. What was I thinking? I loosen my fingers, ready to pull free, when he pivots to face me. He's close enough for his breath to fan my cheek, and his fingers curl around my hand.

Heat sweeps through my body like I just stepped out of an air-conditioned building into the full force of a sunny day. I tilt my chin to look up into his face. His dark eyes glitter with an intensity that makes me weak in the knees.

Sure he's about to kiss me, I tilt my chin up and close my eyes, trying to be brave and embrace the moment. The softest caress brushes my lips, a whispering touch that sends a jolt straight through my center. I can't breathe. I can't think. It's like I'm floating on air, and every cell in my body feels inexplicably alive.

I'm still processing these feelings when the lift chimes and the door spirals open. Tazhio's low voice hums in my ear. "I believe this is your deck."

I open my eyes and see a familiar, fuchsia-carpeted hallway. Yep, this is my floor. My heart is racing. I just met this guy, and I'm about to take him back to my room. I've never dared have a one-night-stand, and I can't believe this is actually going to happen. *With an alien!* Suzanne will be so proud.

Still holding his hand, I step off the lift.

Tazhio's grip tightens briefly around mine as I tug him after me, but he stops at the threshold and gently extracts his fingers. Keeping his gaze on mine, he bows his head. "Have a good rest of your evening."

I blink, suddenly confused as I watch the lift door spiral closed between us.

For several heartbeats, I stare at my own reflection in the metal, trying to understand what just happened. *But he kissed me...*

Oh, God. Had that been a pity kiss? A hot guy like Tazhio probably has ten women a night hit on him, all more elegant than I am.

Face on fire, I glance up and down the hallway, glad to find it empty. No one had seen my embarrassing moment.

Hurrying toward my cabin, I play the scene in the elevator over and over in my head. He had kissed me, right? My eyes had been closed—he could've brushed my lips with his fingertips for all I know. Worse than a pity kiss. *Why, why, why?*

My door slides open automatically, each cabin somehow programmed to recognize the occupant's bio signature, eliminating the problem of losing your keys. I stumble inside, seeing the king-sized bed has been neatly remade after my nap this afternoon. Some sort of candy sits atop the pristine white pillow.

The cabin is nicer than my bedroom at home, but in an art déco sort of way. The vanity has a countertop that looks like it was sliced from the center of a giant pearl, and the bed's silver headboard rises to a gentle peak, also inlaid with what looks like millions of pearls. The walls are covered in a subtle design with overlapping circles and thick lines in shades of pale pink and dove gray that match the slightly darker pink carpet.

Setting Beanie on a puppy pad in the bathroom, I return to the bedroom and pick up the candy, wishing it was ice cream. What I wouldn't do for a pint of Rocky Road at this moment. *I should've known better than to try and be brave.* What a fool he must think me. Tazhio was just doing his job. And I grabbed his hand without asking... My eyes fly open with horror. *Just like that red alien grabbed mine.*

I groan, plopping heavily onto the edge of the bed. *Way to alienate the only alien you found remotely attractive.*

Snorting at my own silent joke, I unwrap the candy. Popping it into my mouth, I let the sweet, melty caramel flavor flood over my tongue. Not ice cream, but still decadent. Maybe I can order ice cream from room service. *I need room service for the entire rest of the cruise.* I dread the thought of showing my face again. Can I pretend to be sick and stay in my cabin for the rest of the trip? I'll absolutely die if I have to face Tazhio again.

Beanie appears carrying his toy moose and sprawls on the carpet near my feet, gnawing happily on one of its antlers. I sigh and lean back on the plush mattress to watch him. "Good thing we like the room, huh, Beanie?"

His little tail wags in agreement.

"I wonder how long it might take to get ice cream delivered." My gaze shifts to my closed cabin door. A diagram on the back of it shows the layout of the ship—all thirteen decks and hundreds of rooms. I frown. "Wait. How did he know which floor my room is on?"

My stomach does flip-flops that have nothing to do with space travel. He can't possibly have memorized the floor every guest is on. But he could've looked me up. Which meant he felt the same zing I did when we first met on the shuttle. *The elevator kiss was real.*

So why did he break away?

I bite my lip, the foggy memory of the ship orientation meeting returning to me. The cruise director instructed us that the aliens would not engage in intimate contact without express verbal consent. What if Tazhio had been waiting for me to invite him to my room? To actually say the words?

After he rescued me from the red alien at the party, he told me to be more assertive about what I want. Yet on the elevator, I did nothing more than smile and take his hand. So he did the decent thing and stayed back.

I flop backward against the mattress and glare up at the ceiling. "Well, shit."

4

TAZHIO

The entire walk back to my quarters, my body is screaming that Tamara is my mate. But I can't tell her that. The Intergalactic Dating Agency will see to it that I never fly again if I attempt to lure a female away from paying guests. Just stepping in with that Fogarian at the party was probably going to have consequences. Worth it though. If I can't have her, I at least want her to be with someone who respects her wishes.

I reach my private quarters and sit stiffly on my bunk. The mirror on the wall across from me shows a familiar yet altered reflection of my features. My shoulders are a bit broader, and my nose slightly less prominent than usual—my matrix's innate response to Tamara's attraction. When a Kirenai finds his mate, his form will intuitively assume the shape his mate prefers, which becomes permanent once they bond.

She makes my shape want to settle.

I lie back on the mattress, remembering the thrill I felt when Tamara threaded her fingers with mine. The nervous yet certain spark of desire in her ocean-gray eyes. The way her breasts swelled above the neckline of her dress as if aching for me to free them.

I ache, as well. Opening the front of my pants, I reach for my excruciatingly hard shaft. As I stroke myself, I imagine myself sliding my palms beneath Tamara's skirt, up her thighs to her center of liquid heat. I pump faster and faster until my breath comes in ragged gasps. The sweet flavor of the feathered kiss still lingers on my lips, like stardust clinging to the hull of the ship.

Sucking in my bottom lip, I imagine her tight pussy dripping with juices. Imagine lapping them up. Imagine her squirming with pleasure as I penetrate her. Her exquisite heat around my cock.

Tamara. My hips buck upward against my hand, and the cascade of my release shakes me from head to toes.

I let my limbs relax and stare up at the gray ceiling, breathing hard. The pressure in my balls is better, but a hollow yearning still aches in my chest. *She's not for you.* No matter what my body is saying, I can't have her. I head to the lavatory, trying to think about other women I've found attractive in the past, hoping to blot her from my mind. As I shower, I end up thinking of Tamara and masturbating again.

"This is ridiculous," I tell my dick as I step out of the stall.

Going to my resting pod, I force my matrix to relax into my natural, amorphous state. I rarely need to rest this deeply, but perhaps if I'm no longer humanoid, my desire for her will subside. When I wake, I'm humanoid again, and my dick is throbbing with thoughts of Tamara. So much for that idea.

I spend the day in my quarters trying to distract myself with some light reading and more not-so-light stroking of my cock. It's all I can do to stay away from tonight's singles party. Jealousy smolders in the pit of my stomach as I imagine Tamara holding someone else's hand at this very moment. Will she take him back to her cabin? Maybe she's holding more than his hand...

Kuzara. These thoughts are driving me crazy. I dig out my bottle of *hahana* liquor, pour a double shot, and sling it back. Before I know it, the bottle is empty, but at least I get drunk enough to fall asleep.

Hung over and grouchy the next morning, I head to the shuttle bay to run diagnostics for my upcoming shuttle tour of the Singing Planet. I settle into the pilot seat and pull up my flight plan. We won't be landing—reaching the surface safely is nearly impossible, but this will be my first non-simulated trip. The magic of the Singing Planet is in its ionosphere. Navigated correctly, the rivers of charged particles will ignite my shuttle into a symphony of sound and light. It is going to be glorious.

I wonder if Tamara signed up for this excursion.

I stare at my console, trying to make sense of the data on the screen, and it takes me a moment to realize I've opened the passenger list over the top of my diagnostics panel, hoping to see her name. *Idiot!* I close the file with a frustrated jab of my finger. It doesn't matter if she'll be on the excursion or not, because I plan to stay in the cockpit the entire time. There is a minimal margin of error for my calculations, and I can't let myself be distracted.

I'm nearly finished calibrating the sensors when Kiozhi's familiar voice floats toward me from the bay. "Tazhio, you in here?"

I call out, "In the cockpit."

My friend ducks inside and glances around the semi-circular bridge area. He's wearing nothing but a pair of short pants that barely cover his crotch. "Don't you ever stop working?" he asks.

I shrug and frown at his clothing. "Why are you naked?"

Kiozhi glances down at himself. "I'm not. These are called swim trunks. All the males on Earth wear them during cruises." He raises both arms and flexes his biceps. "Human females like to see muscles."

I'm struck by a sudden image of Tamara admiring the muscles of other males. Touching them. *Or being touched by them.* A hard lump fills my stomach. "Do the females wear these swim trunks as well?"

"Only at the pool, and they wear a second piece to cover their breasts." Kiozhi makes an appreciative cupping gesture with both hands. "I believe it's called a bikini." He sinks into the co-pilot seat next to me, shoulders slumping. "But I'm not here to talk about that. I found my mate."

I suck in a sharp breath and swivel my chair to face him. I knew he was on this cruise hoping to find a mate, but to be honest, I never actually thought he would. Kiozhi has been a playboy for as long as I've known him. A slow smile spreads across my face. "Wow. Congratulations."

My friend rubs a hand through his hair. Normally, he's excellent at shielding his *Iki'i*, but his frustration fills the cockpit with a grating sensation. "I'm not sure congratulations are in order. I think I made a mistake."

Alarm spikes through me, and my smile drops. Bonding to a female is nothing to be taken lightly. A bond is permanent, linking the pair together and granting the female an extended life to match her mate's. Considering the fact Kirenai lived for hundreds of cycles, a lifetime bond with an unpleasant female could be worse than a prison sentence. "A mistake? How?"

"We met at the first party, and she invited me to her cabin." A dreamy look fills Kiozhi's eyes. "We had the most outrageous sex, but I didn't use my mating shaft. I read that humans like to be courted before bonding, and I was trying to be respectful." He grimaces. "Let me tell you, that was possibly the most willpower I've ever exerted in my life."

I nod in understanding. I know that if I had let things progress with Tamara, we'd probably be mated right now.

Kiozhi continues his story. "The next morning, I sent her flowers with an invitation to join me for lunch. I even reserved the entire forward pool deck just for us." He stares dejectedly at his clenched fists. "She never showed up."

"This is a big ship. Maybe she just didn't know how to find you?" I offer. On one hand, I understand his distress, but on the other, at least he's allowed to pursue her.

His palpable frustration twists to something more painful. "I wondered that, too, so I had the gift shop send a box of something called chocolates to her room and told her I would pick her up for dinner. She returned the chocolates." He bares his teeth in a snarl. "And the next time I saw her, she was at the karaoke bar with another male, singing her heart out about love."

"Ouch." I cringe. Thank the gods I'd stayed away from the parties and seeing Tamara doing something like that. "I'm sorry. But at least you didn't bond with her. That would make it a hundred times worse."

"You don't understand. She's the one. I know it." Kiozhi's expression is pained. "I know she felt our connection. My *Iki'i* can't lie." He leans forward, gaze intent. "I've been reading about human courting games where mates try to make one another jealous by pretending disinterest. I believe this must be her intention, and I need your help coming up with a plan to win her."

I'd seen my friend with plenty of women, but never obsessed with one like this. *He's as tormented as I am.* There must be something about human females that turns men into idiots. I shake my head. "These humans can be intoxicating, but you need to face reality. If she's spurning your advances, I don't think she's your mate."

"Humans don't recognize their mates right away. If she would just spend some time with me, she'd figure it out."

"You can't force her to spend time with you."

"She's all I can think about," Kiozhi says between clenched teeth.

"I know the feeling." The words are out before I can stop them.

Kiozhi's eyes narrow to slits. "You found a female?"

A painful knot in my chest keeps me from saying it out loud, so I nod. I pat the instrument panel, thinking about how he told me I work too much. "You need to find something else to think about. Like me."

But my friend won't let it go. "Did you meet her at the party?"

"It doesn't matter. The guests are off limits to the crew."

"*Kuzara*, who cares? When you find your true mate, don't let anything stand in your way."

"She's not meant to be mine. The IDA genetically profiled her to match one or more of the guests. She has other males to choose from, just like your female is also investigating other options. Let her go and move on."

"Did you sleep with her?" Kiozhi persists.

"Of course not! I told you, she's off limits." I swivel back toward my console. "The only solution is to find something else to focus on. The excursion to the Singing Planet is today. You should come. It's going to be amazing."

Kiozhi rubs the back of his neck. "This is the trip you've been talking about? The one you just got certified to do?"

"Yes. I've been studying the frequencies the different ionic layers will create—"

"Yes, yes, I know. You're going to play a song with the shuttle. Once-in-a-lifetime experience and all that." Kiozhi taps his chin. "I wonder if Suzanne would agree to view it with me?"

I sigh. "The point is for you to get your mind *off* the female. You should come alone."

"I don't do things alone." Kiozhi scowls.

"You know what I mean. There will be plenty of other female guests there. Or if you prefer, I'll let you sit up here with me in the co-pilot seat."

Kiozhi drums his fingers on his thigh, then stands. "Fine. I'll come along. But I expect this to be the best concert I've ever been to."

"It will be, I promise."

Once Kiozhi is gone, I resume my diagnostic checks. This excursion is going to blow everyone's mind and help us stop brooding over these intoxicating females once and for all.

5

TAMARA

"*I* swear to God it's like you and Suzanne swapped bodies," Jennifer says as we step onto the lift headed to the shuttle bay. "We started this trip with her all gung-ho to party and now she hides in her room half the day, while you swore up and down you planned to be a hermit and now you want to come on an excursion." She loops one arm through mine. "Not that I'm complaining. I think it's great you're coming out of your shell, plus your phone will be really helpful collecting data."

I smile nervously without answering. The moving elevator just made my stomach swoop, and I have to swallow back lunch. How am I going to endure another shuttle ride?

Over the past few days, I've joined every onboard activity that came my way, hoping to bump into Tazhio again. I've strolled along every aisle in the gambling area with its flashing lights and strange gaming tables. I've eaten at every restaurant, much to Bethany's delight. I've even had drinks at the poolside bar with its dizzying view of the stars.

I never once spotted Tazhio among the masses of blue aliens spread across the ship. I was beginning to wonder if he altered his shape just to avoid me until Jennifer pointed out that I've been looking in the wrong places. He's a pilot, so the most likely place to find him is in the shuttle.

Now I just have to get through this excursion without embarrassing myself by besmirching the steward's well-polished shoes.

The lift opens on the shuttle bay, and I hesitate, one hand inside my purse to touch Beanie's comforting warmth. My heart is racing a mile a minute as I take in the familiar purple shuttle resting in the middle of the cavernous bay. Beyond the shuttle, mechanics with tools hanging off their belts move about, glancing up from their work at the arrival of guests. High above, the entire ceiling glows as if it's made of one solid light fixture, and spherical drones flit back and forth.

Just outside the lift, a steward who looks like a classic Area 51 alien with gray-green skin and huge black eyes stands at a podium. He—or she, I'm not certain how to tell the difference or if gender is even binary for these aliens—is speaking with a pair of well-muscled blue aliens in swim trunks.

Jennifer elbows me, and we exchange a smirk. Many of the aliens had taken to wearing the singular item of clothing, and while most women don't seem to mind all the man-candy strutting around, I've felt a little awkward at the more formal evening events.

"Are you here for the Singing Planet excursion?" the steward asks.

Jennifer nods and gives our names.

"More Bloom sisters! How delightful," the steward says with a wide smile. My sisters and I have gained some notoriety among the aliens as siblings traveling together. The small alien points toward a path marked by red velvet ropes leading to the shuttle. "Your other party member is already here. Please have an enjoyable trip!"

Near the shuttle ramp, I spot Suzanne wrapped in a pastel swirl scarf and sunglasses. She's hiding behind a blue-skinned porter in a white crew uniform next to Jennifer's enormous astronomy case. At the first party on board, she hooked up with someone who is now obsessed with her, and she's trying to avoid running into him.

I search the mechanics and other personnel for any sign of Tazhio as we follow the path between the velvet ropes, my flip-flops slapping my heels. Lunch feels like a rock in my stomach. I absolutely knew it was a mistake to eat right before the trip, but Jennifer was hungry and I'm a nervous eater, so I gave in. I keep one hand inside my purse against Beanie's furry shoulders.

What if Tazhio really is avoiding me on purpose? What if he never comes out of the cockpit? *What if I spend the entire flight in the bathroom barfing?*

Seeming to sense my worry, Jennifer again loops her arm through mine. "You'll be fine. You've been on the ship for days now and haven't thrown up. The motion sickness patch is working."

I nod, praying that remains true on a flight that's advertised as a "ride of a lifetime."

"Where have you been?" Suzanne hisses the moment we're within earshot. "Vin Diesel and I have been waiting for at least ten minutes." She gestures toward the big blue porter who's been Jennifer's shadow since we arrived.

I bite back a grin. The guy does look sort of like Vin Diesel, right down to his bald head.

Jennifer scowls, a flush creeping into her cheeks. "Be polite. His name's Nazhin."

The porter's features remain emotionless, but as always, his silvery eyes are locked on Jennifer. "I requested an exclusive spot in the viewing area for you and your equipment," he says.

"Thank you so much." Jennifer smiles and looks around the area expectantly. "Where's Bethany?"

Suzanne rolls her eyes. "She bailed on us. Busy teaching an alien how to bake a birthday cake or something." She lowers her sunglasses just enough to focus directly on me over the dark lenses. "I'm surprised you didn't find an excuse not to come, Tamara. You must really have the hots for this pilot."

"Shh!" I glance toward the open shuttle and duck behind the tall porter, heat rising to my cheeks. My older sister has no shame when it comes to men.

She grins at me and moves toward the ramp. "Let's get inside before I'm spotted."

Jennifer follows, with Nazhin carrying her gear.

I take a few deep breaths to calm myself before joining them. My stomach is tangled up with dread and hope and a whole lot of other feelings that keep rising into my throat. *What the hell am I doing?* Tazhio's way out of my league. He's not only good looking, he's a pilot. Maybe I should forget all about this right now, before it's too late and I ruin the trip for everyone.

A familiar voice booms my name across the shuttle bay. "Tamara! I've been looking for you everywhere!"

I cringe, recognizing the voice of my crimson-haired admirer from the first night on the *Romantasy*. The squat alien is barreling down the path between the velvet ropes, wearing nothing but a Speedo. Apparently, his crimson hair grows other places on his body, as well. *Crap.*

Why is this guy so determined to win me over? I hurry to the ramp. Maybe I can get a seat between my sisters where the alien can't pester me. But Nazhin is blocking the way with Jennifer's load of equipment.

Heavy footfalls pound up the ramp behind me. "I would be honored to have you sit with me," the squat alien booms, slightly out of breath. He comes to a halt with the bare, heated skin of his shoulder brushing my arm, then takes a tiny step back—he's been careful about making physical contact after Tazhio's intervention. But his eyes are nearly level with my breasts, and he seems to have no clue that's not where he should be looking.

I edge sideways. "Thank you, no. I'm with my sisters."

He lifts his gaze to mine, smiling to reveal two rows of pointed teeth. "We can make room for them, too. I've been on this tour before and have reserved a block of the very best seats."

Just then Nazhin clears the doorway, and my heartbeat bursts into a gallop. Tazhio stands at the top of the ramp.

His gaze locks with mine. "Tamara, your VIP seat is ready."

VIP seat? I don't know what he means, but I'm not going to argue. Nodding dumbly, I ignore the spluttering alien beside me and follow Tazhio inside. Suzanne spots me from her seat in the passenger area and grins broadly, giving me a thumbs up.

Heat flushes through my body, and I grin back before turning to follow Tazhio through the circular door into the cockpit. I can't believe this is happening. Not only have I found him, I now know he wasn't ignoring me. Plus, he's offering me a special seat. *Maybe he likes me after all.*

The cockpit is about the size of a small bedroom, with two bucket seats facing what I assume are control panels and a large view screen showing the doors of the shuttle bay. One chair is occupied by another blue alien wearing a cream-colored tunic belted at the waist, green pants, and tall black boots that remind me of a pirate.

He takes me in with raised eyebrows and shoots to his feet. "Aren't you one of the Bloom sisters?"

I nod, too nervous to speak. Sweat has blossomed beneath my arms and I hope it isn't showing through my turquoise blouse.

Tazhio rubs the back of his neck. "Um, would you mind if Tamara took your seat?"

It registers that this guy isn't in a crew uniform. Is Tazhio booting someone for my sake? That seems unfair. I back up a step. "I don't mean to intrude. I can go sit with my sisters."

"No, no, I'm more than happy to exchange seats." The booted alien gestures toward the chair, then squeezes past me with a grin. In the blink of an eye, he's gone, and the door spirals closed. Tazhio stands there a moment, looking at me expectantly.

Nausea rolls through my gut. This is a mistake. The only thing this is going to accomplish is embarrassing me in front of a handsome guy. I turn to look for the door handle. "I'm not sure this is a good idea."

A steward's voice enters the cockpit over the intercom. "Everyone's on board, sir. I'm securing the ramp."

Tazhio puts a hand to my lower back, sending delicious tingles up my spine as he urges me forward. "Too late to change your mind now. Please, sit."

Breathing shallowly, I sink onto the seat, keeping my purse on my lap like a shield. Beanie pokes his head from the top and whines. I stroke between his ears. "It's okay, everything's okay."

Tazhio takes the other chair, and his deft fingers play over the symbols on his console. On the view screen, I watch the shuttle bay doors spiral open. Through the faint glitter of what I assume must be a force-field looms a glowing yellow planet with a band of multi-colored rings.

Oh, shit.

The shuttle rises from the deck and shoots forward into space. My stomach flip-flops, and I grip the arms of the seat. *Oh, God, oh God.*

6

TAZHIO

I guide the shuttle out of the bay toward the glowing, multi-colored rings of the Singing Planet, hyper-conscious of Tamara in the co-pilot seat nearby. The moment I heard her voice on the boarding ramp, Kiozhi sensed my sudden alertness and insisted I at least greet her. When I saw that Fogarian pestering her again, I knew I couldn't leave her on her own in the passenger cabin.

Now she's sitting at my side for this momentous flight. *What if fate threw us together, after all?*

The problem is, her anxiety is getting to me. Sharp and stabbing, it's enough to give me the onset of a headache. If it's this bad for me, it must be excruciating for her.

Her eyes are squeezed shut, and she's frantically petting her quadruped's small head with a trembling hand. The quadruped seems to absorb her anxiety as it looks up at her with huge, liquid eyes, but her tension is overwhelming.

"I'm an excellent pilot and trained extensively for this tour," I reassure her. "You have nothing to worry about. I promise."

She cracks one eye to look at me. "I believe you. I get motion sick is all."

Motion sick. I'd read about the phenomenon as part of the emergency medical training the crew took to prepare for hosting human guests. I recite the diagnosis, "A condition where humans experience a malfunction of the vestibular system resulting in dizziness, nausea, and vomiting."

"Um, yes." She claps one hand over her mouth.

I frown. I need to ease her discomfort or she'll never want to fly with me again.

Since it's a straight shot between the *Romantasy* and the planet, I put the shuttle on temporary autopilot and swivel in my seat to face her. "I believe I can help. Give me your hands."

Her cheeks have a greenish hue, but she pulls her hand from her mouth and hesitantly extends it toward me, keeping the other on her quadruped.

"I'll need both hands if your symbiote will allow."

She blinks in confusion until I gesture toward the small animal in her lap.

"Oh, my dog," she says. "Right." Picking up the creature, she sets it on the floor next to her feet, along with her purse. "Stay, Beanie."

The dog—I will have to remember that word—stands and puts its tiny front paws on her leg. She seems to find comfort in the creature, so I don't interfere.

Taking both of her wrists, I open my *Iki'i*, searching for specific pain receptors beneath her delicate skin. She is so soft and warm, and her perfume reminds me of *malila* flowers opening under the moonlight. I yearn to press my mouth against her palms and feather kisses up her arms, to bury my face in her bright copper hair and pull her lush body against mine.

I shake my head free of those thoughts. She is suffering, and here I am thinking like a rutting *ijin'en.* Locating the correct nerves on her wrists, I press my thumbs into her flesh. "Please tell me if I press too hard."

She shakes her head, her ocean-gray eyes fixed on mine. "I'm okay."

The shorts she wears leave her knees bare, exposing her freckled skin. I can't help but wonder how far up her legs those adorable freckles continue and have to force my attention back to her face. "My medical training said to hold this until the patient finds relief."

A flicker of awe courses through her. "Wow, you're a pilot and a doctor?"

I chuckle. "No. All crew members are trained to treat minor human ailments. We want to be certain everyone has a comfortable and pleasant trip."

She bites her bottom lip and glances away, her cheeks flushing pink. "Of course. That makes sense. It's your job."

A new flavor of anxiety floods my *Iki'i.* Embarrassment? Her capricious flow of emotions is hard to keep up with. "I take no offense," I assure her.

"You're too kind." She lifts her eyes back to mine and squares her shoulders. "I need to apologize for what happened in the elevator. I'm sure I put you in an uncomfortable position."

I suck in a breath. Does she somehow know that I've had my hand down my pants for the last three days? My dick has been half-hard from the moment I heard her voice outside the shuttle, and now it surges to full attention. *She can't know what I've been doing.* Can she? My heart fills my throat, and I wonder if I might've missed some information about humans having telepathy.

Just then, a breathy note of sound passes through the shuttle, and motes of white light dance in the air between us.

"*Kuzara!*" Releasing her arms, I spin back to the console. I nearly forgot we're on approach, and we've already entered the first ionized rings of the Singing Planet.

I disengage the auto-pilot, check the sensors, and level the shuttle's orbit. Timing is crucial for this excursion, and we've entered the planet's ionosphere out of phase. *I can adjust.*

"We're okay," I say, as much for my benefit as Tamara's. But I haven't even engaged the safety restraints yet, let alone prepared the passengers and crew for what's coming. I activate the restraint system, and the seat softens and molds around my body like a harness. I know the same thing is happening to passengers ship-wide.

Tamara gasps. "Oh, God, what's happening?"

The other passengers are likely wondering the same thing, so I open the comm. "This is your captain. I've engaged the safety features of your seats. It's normal to encounter some turbulence during this excursion, so please remain seated until you've been released."

A note like a woman's sigh courses over the hull.

I had an entire script memorized to introduce the tour, but now that we're already immersed, I'll have to cut it short. "Welcome to one of the few known wonders of the galaxy—the Singing Planet. Please sit back and enjoy this symphony of sound and light."

Adjusting our course toward an eddy of ionized particles ahead, I modulate the shielding to complement the frequency. Golden streamers caress the view screen, and a high, sweet chord vibrates through the hull. Pleasure courses through me. This is exactly what I planned for the excursion's first note.

Tamara's posture relaxes, and she whispers, "It's so beautiful."

Her anxiety is gone, consumed by pure wonder.

My *Iki'i* thrums with joy, and I take a breath, letting the mix of sensations wash through me. I've flown countless simulations of the Singing Planet, but the real thing is ten times more astounding, especially when shared with the charming female beside me. I can't help grinning. "It's only going to get better."

I guide the shuttle deeper into the ionosphere, creating a wavering alto that vibrates the deck beneath our feet. Flashing motes of aquamarine join the streamers of golden light, merge, and form rings of emerald green. I glance at Tamara.

Her dog is back on her lap, curled into a furry ball, and she's smiling and holding out one hand as if trying to touch the light. When a wide emerald band seems to slip down her arm like a bracelet, Tamara laughs, the sound as pleasing as the note now gliding along the hull.

Pride fills my chest. I never realized how much I would enjoy seeing someone else's response to the show. *Tamara's response.*

A brassy note creeps into the melody, and I quickly adjust course to avoid a hotspot. The gravitational stabilizers take a second to compensate, and I sense Tamara's nausea rising again. *Pay attention*, I tell myself, though her upset stomach will be the least of our concerns if the shuttle gets mired in heavy ionization. The trick to flying around the Singing Planet is to keep to the shallow currents and take advantage of eddies that will help shed excess ionization on the hull.

The twisting particle-rivers braid themselves into a complicated map, and I merge our trajectory alongside a new current. A wavering chord vibrates through the hull like the fragile wings of a *lonala* moth. Satisfied, I once more chance a look in Tamara's direction.

Sparkling rosy light bathes her pale, freckled skin. "This is the most amazing thing I've ever seen." She grabs her purse and pulls out a small flat device. "I should use Jennifer's new app to record this."

Purple and red light explode like fireworks against the view screen, and I again check our course as the song dips into a low, rumbling moan. Some sort of anomaly has appeared on the sensors. I adjust course, but then my console flickers. The anomaly disappears, only to resurface directly in front of us. *What the* kuzara *is happening?*

Before I can again change direction, the console flickers and goes dark. My hands freeze over the surface for a heartbeat before my training kicks in. I stand up and move over to access the copilot console in front of Tamara.

It's dead too.

"*Kuzara.*" I look over my shoulder at Tamara.

She's gaping back at me. The thing she called a phone is clutched loosely in her hand, human symbols scrolling across its screen. The security team had cleared human technology as non-threatening to our systems, but the device is the only thing I can think of that might interfere with the controls.

"Stop what you're doing." I reach for the phone just as the gravitational stabilizers cut out. The deck lurches out from under me, and I stumble backward, slamming to a stop against the view screen.

Tamara screams, echoed by muted shouting from the passenger cabin. Her fear floods my senses, a drowning wave of panic that momentarily blinds me. I shut down my *Iki'i* to keep from being overwhelmed.

Gravity stabilizes, and I lurch back toward my seat. "Turn off that device!"

The entire shuttle is shaking and rocking, and the music of the Singing Planet has turned into a monstrous roar.

Tapping frantically at the device, Tamara holds up the now dark screen for me to see. "It's off!"

I drop into the captain's seat, glad for the instant grip of the safety restraint as the shuttle jerks sideways. My sensors are rebooting, startup commands flowing across the console. Even without any sensor readings, my instincts tell me we must be caught in one of the heavy ion currents, but I have no way of gauging the shuttle's direction, especially with several huge, pulsing ruptures flashing against the view screen.

Emergency protocols rattle through my mind, and I slam one hand against the emergency beacon while using the other to increase the strength of the safety restraints. The seat cushions soften further, wrapping up and around my legs and torso but leaving my arms free. The restraints in the passenger cabin will encase each passenger completely and act as life pods in the event of a crash.

I check on Tamara, relieved to see she's well secured and clutching both arms around her dog, although her skin looks pale as ice and her features are creased in a grimace of terror.

My console finishes rebooting, and coldness fills my body. The shuttle has entered the planet's stratosphere in an uncontrolled spin. How did we travel so far off course? I engage full thrusters, trying to regain control, but heavy ionization must already have clogged the engines.

The view ahead coalesces into roiling storm clouds. Warnings flash over my console and across the view screen. The shuttle is nearing the atmosphere, and hull temperature is rising. We'll burn up unless I redirect all power to the shields—which means no power for thrusters. No chance of pulling out of this dive.

We are going to crash.

I grit my teeth, boost the shields, and brace for impact. *So much for impressing Tamara with my piloting skills.*

7

TAMARA

I grip Beanie against my chest, watching the view screen in horror. My stomach has been left somewhere behind, but I'm too terrified to be sick. Clouds of shifting color create what would've been a spectacular show if it wasn't for the agonizing screech of sound coursing through the ship. As the shuttle bucks and spins, the seat holds me in place, my own weight crushing the breath from my body.

Tazhio taps at the control panel in front of his seat, teeth bared in a grimace. Blinding sparks cover the view screen, and for a moment, I'm terrified we've caught on fire. Then what appears to be the top of a storm-tossed sea of deep green leaves materializes between the flashes of light.

"Shields are down! Brace for impact!" shouts Tazhio as the shuttle plows into the canopy.

Huge branches slam against the hull, and a tearing sound rips through the cabin. The next thing I know, I'm no longer surrounded by walls, but being buffeted by wind and debris.

Seat still clamped around me like a glove, I hurtle through darkness and trees.

Falling. Spinning.

Leaves as big as serving platters whip by, forcing me to close my eyes and turn my head to keep from being blinded. Pain sears across my knee. I squeeze my eyes tighter and clutch Beanie against my chest. I pray I'm not crushing him to death, but I know if I let go he'll be hurtled like a missile.

Suddenly, my seat slams into something behind me.

And the world goes dark.

8

TAMARA

I'm dreaming about a cozy cabin in the woods with a lumberjack making me pancakes when a strange hooting note brings me awake. I open my eyes to a rainbow of glowing plants and mushrooms, mostly green or purple, with a few clumps of hot-pink and sparkling yellow leaves interspersed among them. The plants seem to be the only light source, creating a sort of murky green haze to see by. I realize I'm no longer in the shuttle seat, but sprawled out on a mattress of leaves with fuzzy undersides as thick and soft as a fleece blanket.

In a rush, the horrific, hurtling fall from the shuttle comes back to me. I sit up, head spinning, and search for my dog. "Beanie?"

Chittering and hooting and other strange jungle noises are all that answer.

Where is everyone? Taking a few calming breaths, I notice that my left shin is wrapped in a leaf, small vines neatly tied around it to keep it in place. Someone has been here with me, then. I peek under the leaf and wince at the sight of a long gash caked with some sort of green goo that smells oddly like maple syrup. *Well, that explains my hunger for pancakes.*

I survey the glowing plants again. "Hello, is anyone here?"

When no one answers, I stand up, body aching with what feels like a million bruises. I've lost my flip-flops, and the cut on my leg throbs. It turns out I'm standing in a pit about as deep as my shoulders, with shrubbery growing up the sides. As far as I can see, gnarled, purple-gray trunks as thick as redwoods rise into the air. The glowing vegetation grows like moss up the trunks, fading into a dark canopy where long, glowing vines dangle from branches like a creepy rendition of a Tarzan cartoon.

"Jennifer! Suzanne!" The thick jungle swallows my voice. "Tazhio? Anyone out there?"

I think I can hear faint barking in the distance. My heart constricts. Who knows what kind of trouble my baby might be in? "Beanie, I'm coming!"

Using the plants as handholds, I pull myself over the edge of the pit onto my belly. The ground dips into another hollow a few feet away, and I realize the entire forest floor is a roiling mass of tangled roots.

Shaking with nerves, I get to my feet. The root is rough under my bare feet, but not unbearable. A surprisingly strong breeze rushes between the trees, making the curtain of vines overhead dance and sway. Butted up against one of the massive trunks nearby, the crumpled remains of our shuttle rests at the end of a swathe of carnage carved into the ground. Pieces of shuttle debris are scattered along the trench. One of the chairs from the shuttle is wedged in a smaller hollow nearby. There's nobody in it, so I think it might be the one I was in.

God, how am I even alive? And what has happened to everyone else?

"Hello?" I call again into the forest.

Beanie yips, a frantic sound that makes my chest tighten.

"I'm coming!" I call back, examining the gouged trench behind the shuttle. The root I'm standing on snakes in a sort of raised trail alongside the debris. It's as good a path as any, so I take a step. I haven't gone too far before I realize my feet aren't as tough as I first thought, but I can't be a wimp, so I find a broken branch to use as a walking stick and keep going.

I follow the trench, climbing over twisted roots and avoiding a patch of slimy looking mushrooms as I make my way toward Beanie's sporadic barking. The forest muffles the sound and makes it impossible to guess how far away he might be. *Please let him be with the others.*

I pause for breath near a giant pool nestled between the roots. The inky depths of the water reflect glowing fairy plants dotting the banks, and if I hadn't been in such dire circumstances, I would've snapped a photo. Then I remember my phone might be what landed us in this mess to begin with—most likely Jennifer's stupid, amped up astronomy app, since that's what was running when the trouble began. *When I find her, I'm going to kill her.* Then I add, *Please, God, let me find her and Suzanne.*

Beanie barks again, and I plant my walking stick, mincing carefully across the rough bark. I'm almost past the pool when an enormous pair of bulbous eyes emerges from the water right next to me.

"Oh, shit!" I take a surprised step back, lose my footing, and topple backwards down into the shuttle trench.

I land on my back; the wind knocked out of me. As I lay stunned at the bottom, it hits home that I'm on an alien planet. There might be creatures here who want to eat me, or toxic plants, or hell, there could be toxic plants that want to eat me. And what about Beanie? He's so tiny and helpless.

Sitting up, I scream, "Beanie, come!"

Something resembling a gargantuan centipede rises over the edge of the embankment where I've fallen, shiny and black and dripping water. Its bulging eyes are definitely focused straight at me.

My pulse goes into overdrive, and I roll to my knees, scrambling toward the opposite side of the trench. I beeline it toward a jagged sheet of purple hull material as wide as a queen-sized bed that's leaning against the wall. I think I might be able to hide underneath it. The jagged edge digs into my shoulder and tears my shirt, but I won't fit.

Spinning, I see the centipede's long body descending over the edge of the trench. My heart hammers against my breastbone. I lost my walking stick when I fell, so I search the ground for another weapon. There's nothing nearby except dirt and leaves.

The thing is coming straight toward me.

"Get away! Shoo!" I pick up a clod of dirt and hurl it as hard as I can. I don't think a shower of dirt will actually be able to stop the creature, but something hard thunks loudly against the beast's body and it shudders. More thuds follow, though I'm no longer throwing anything.

Suddenly, the creature stops moving and coils into a tight ball a mere few feet from where I stand. I gape at it. *What's happening?*

Snarls and grunts erupt behind me, and four-legged creatures that remind me of giant, human-sized ferrets swarm down the bank toward the monster. Rising onto their hind legs, they circle the centipede and begin jabbing it with what appear to be crude knives. Though they arrived on four legs, their front paws seem quite adept as hands, and I now notice they each wear a thick belt strung with what might be more weapons.

One of them turns its beady-eyed attention to me, its muzzle splitting into a grin that reveals blunt gray teeth. Leaving its knife embedded in the centipede's carcass, it holds both hands out to me as it chitters and purrs. *It's trying to communicate.*

I don't know if the sounds it's making are actual words, but I reply anyway. Maybe the universal translator they injected me with when we boarded the *Romantasy* will help. "God, thank you so much."

Then I catch sight of what can only be a glistening pink erection jutting from between the ferret alien's legs. It steps closer purring, "Fffffffeeeeem."

Dread clamps my insides as I suddenly get the distinct impression he wants to stab me with something other than his spear. I take an unsteady step backward and raise both hands. "Stop right there."

The other four ferret aliens stop stabbing the centipede and turn to me, all sporting similar bright pink erections. Their muzzles are split in toothy snarls—or perhaps leers? Good God, getting murdered by a giant centipede would be awful, but gang-raped by a bunch of giant ferret aliens will be horrific. I look around frantically, once more in search of a weapon. The trench wall rises sharply behind me, impossible to climb.

"Help!" I scream, hoping someone from the shuttle might hear me as I edge sideways, hoping for a chance to run. "Anyone, please!"

The ferret alien keeps pace while stroking his erection with one six-fingered hand. He reaches toward me with the other.

That's it. If he touches me, I'm done for. I turn to run, but discover one of the others has already flanked me. "Shit."

He thrusts a severed centipede leg under my nose, purring and spouting more syllables. The leg is floppy, more like a tentacle than a bug's leg. Viscous fluid drips from the severed end, flooding the air with a scent like sour milk.

My stomach churns, and bile rises to my throat.

Thankfully, the first alien doesn't like competition. He growls and tries to snatch the leg from his competitor, who jerks his arm back to keep his prize. They fall on each other, snarling and wrestling for possession of the item.

But there's still no hope of escape. The other three aliens are already pressing past the fight, chittering and purring. Their pink penises jut straight at me, and each of them holds a dismembered centipede leg toward me like some sort of obscene offering.

"No, thank you," I choke out. I step backward, my ass against the trench wall. Tazhio's words about being more assertive return to me, so I stand up straighter. "I don't want them. Leave me alone."

The ferret aliens seem undeterred. One sticks the severed end of his centipede leg into his mouth and sucks loudly, then offers it to me again. Another waves his trophy under my nose, spattering my face with centipede ooze. It adheres to my skin with the scent of sour milk and pus.

My stomach heaves. Unable to hold back any longer, I double over, spewing vomit.

The aliens growl and back up.

Eyes watering, I wipe centipede ooze from my cheeks. But I'm relieved to see the ferret aliens seem put off. Their erections have softened and they're now talking and gesturing to each other as if arguing. For once, my sensitive stomach may actually turn out to be beneficial.

I breathe shallowly through my mouth and inch sideways along the trench wall, hoping to slip away.

No such luck. Two of the aliens remove coils of rope from their belts and advance toward me.

"Stay the fuck back!" I clutch my stomach as if I might puke again.

But the surprise has worn off, it seems. In three quick steps, they grab me.

"Stop! Help!" I slap at their hands, but they drive me to the ground. Within moments, they have me strung up like a stuck pig and are carrying me across the trench.

9

TAZHIO

I pause next to an enormous purple-black branch blocking my path. Shattered twigs and crushed leaves lay scattered around the broken limb, and more loose foliage continues to flutter down from the damaged canopy. I've been searching the hollows and swells of the forest floor for hours now, but still can't find any sign of survivors. At this rate, I fear it will take days to find everyone.

At least Tamara is safe. I'd manually ejected the co-pilot seat when we started breaking apart, and I'd located her near the shuttle remains. Aside from a minor cut on one leg, she isn't injured, but she's unconscious. I don't want to leave her, but as the pilot, I'm responsible for all the passengers, not just Tamara.

When the shields failed, the shuttle's passenger seats jettisoned, scattering the life pods across the forested landscape. I'd guided the nose of the shuttle between the massive trunks, trying to minimize the damage. The impact with the ground gouged a wide path through the tangled roots, and the remains of the shuttle now lie crumpled against a tree. I only survived because of my Kirenai abilities.

The lump in my chest rises to my throat again as I think of our future. I'm not looking forward to telling everyone that there's little chance of a rescue. I can count on one hand the number of ships that have made it safely on and off this planet's surface. The ionic storms encasing the atmosphere block communication to or from the ground, which means sensors will be hard-pressed to locate the crash. And even if sensors do manage to find us, finding a pilot willing to brave the storms is another matter.

I watch a miniature tornado spin over the glowing shrubbery nearby, a vortex of rainbow-colored leaves. The brisk wind sweeping in from above is testament to the perpetual storm chewing the upper atmosphere, and I'm worried the debris from our crash will continue to rain down on the area. We'll have to set up camp well away from the shuttle's path to be sure we remain safe.

A familiar bit of cloth hidden beneath the debris catches my attention. Tamara's bag. My heart plummets. What if her dog's still inside? It hadn't been with Tamara when I found her still encased in her seat, and I was too busy piloting the shuttle to pay attention to what happened to the creature during the crash. But I know the dog considers the bag its home.

Hurrying over, I dig the bag free and pull it open. No dog, just some tufts of shed fur. Both relief and disappointment roll through me. I'd hate to have to tell Tamara her dog is dead, but I also hate to tell her it's still missing. The device Tamara called a phone is inside, along with several other objects I don't recognize, so I loop the bag over one shoulder and continue searching.

I'm attempting to climb over a large root when a faint whine reaches me, barely more than a whimper. The few intrepid explorers who'd successfully visited this planet reported the local wildlife as benign unless antagonized, but it is always best to stay alert. I drop back to the ground and sharpen my *Iki'i*, raking my attention over the bushes.

Huddling beneath a clump of glowing yellow leaves, I spot a familiar, furry quadruped. The poor thing is emanating terror, and I can't see it well enough to tell if it's injured. How it survived the fall so far from where Tamara and her padded seat landed is beyond me.

Right now, all that's important is that the dog is alive, and Tamara will be happy. Smiling, I lower the bag to the ground and hold it open for Beanie to enter. "Come on," I coax. "Let's go see Tamara."

The tiny creature backs deeper into the glowing leaves, still wary.

Using my *Iki'i* to radiate calm, I coax, "It's okay. You're safe with me."

The dog barks and dances away, wariness becoming more playful.

I'm glad it doesn't appear injured, but after several minutes chasing the agile creature, my relief sours to frustration. I sit on a gnarled stump and glare at the dog.

Tiny pink tongue sticking out in a mocking grin, the dog yips once and pants happily.

"You're wilier than an escaped *nezumi*," I grumble, thinking about a rodent-like pet I had as a child. Now I understand why my mother hated that thing. I don't have time for this. I stand. "That's it. I'm done chasing you. There are people out there who need me. Follow me or don't."

I shoulder Tamara's bag and turn away. The faint sound of a familiar female voice reaches me on the wind. "Help, please!"

It's coming from where I left Tamara. *Kuzara, I should've stayed with her!*

I pelt between the trees, leaping over twisted roots and glowing shrubs. It takes several minutes to reach the crash site. How did I manage to wander so far? I burst from the glowing brush next to the shuttle trench. On the far side, a group of furred humanoids are chittering rapidly among themselves. Between them, they carry three horizontal poles strung with what look like dead carcasses.

My stomach twists with dread. *No!*

Then one carcass squirms, and Tamara's hoarse voice shouts, "Untie me!"

Without another thought, I leap down into the trench. "Tamara!"

"Tazhio!" She writhes against her bindings. "Help me!"

The humanoids turn, dropping the poles with their burdens.

I hear Tamara grunt as she hits the ground. I don't know if any of the other poles hold passengers, but that doesn't matter. Tamara is alive, and I intend to keep her that way.

One humanoid brandishes a primitive knife, while several others yank slingshots from their belts. They chitter a string of syllables my universal translator can't understand, but I'm fairly certain they aren't saying anything nice.

I force myself to pull back on my rage. This is a first contact situation, and my job is to be diplomatic. Starting out with bloodshed will only cause ongoing trouble for the survivors, which is the last thing I want if we're forced to stay here long term. But it's all I can do not to rip out their throats and wrest Tamara from captivity.

My universal translator will pick up on the language once it receives enough input—I just need to exercise patience. So I cease my advance and hold up both hands in the universal sign of peace. "I am peaceful," I say slowly. "A friend."

They rally to block Tamara from sight where she lies tied up on the ground. Strong possessive waves strike my open *Iki'i* like physical blows. I know it will hinder my translator's learning process, but I shield my senses. If this keeps up, I'm going to do something I can't take back.

I point slowly toward Tamara. "She's with me. Let her go."

The tallest of the humanoids growls a few syllables, and a bright pink phallus springs upright between his legs. The others' penises also spring to life, and the tall one pumps his hips suggestively, baring blunt gray teeth.

I'm a pilot, not a biologist, but I do like to read, and I know there are many species who use physical posturing to measure status. With a sinking feeling, I realize these beings are probably using the size of their genitals to communicate rank. If I want to speak their language, I have no choice but to respond in kind.

Hardly believing what I'm about to do, I drop Tamara's bag and unzip my flight suit, shrugging it from my shoulders. Standing tall, I will my crotch into a massive erection.

Several of the humanoids grunt, and one strokes his shaft as if trying to coax it into a more competitive size.

Thrusting my hips forward, I say, "The female is mine."

Tamara pauses her wriggling and emits a strangled gasp.

"Ffffeeemal ours." The tall humanoid growls and puffs out his chest. More words follow, too fast for my translator to catch.

A projectile hits me from one of the humanoids's slingshots. The impact isn't painful, but a round yellow object that looks like a burr or a spiny nutshell covered in wicked spines now sticks to my chest. I pluck it free, and it leaves behind a sticky residue. The muscle beneath turns numb, and I realize they must be using some sort of toxin or paralytic.

I harden my matrix just as more spiny projectiles head my way. Though I'm feeling the effects of the first strike, I'm impervious to the rest of them, and the initial numbness doesn't seem to be spreading any farther.

Keeping my gaze steady on the tall one I assume is the leader, I thrust my hips again and say, "You cannot hurt me. Return the female and we'll be on our way."

Instead of handing her over, the leader and one other grab Tamara's pole and dart into the brush.

"Tazhio!" she screams.

"*Kuzara.*" I start forward, but the flight suit is still tangled around my ankles. I kick free, shouting, "Bring her back!"

The three remaining humanoids continue to fire, fanning out to flank me. They've dropped to four legs and move with fluid grace over the rough terrain, quicker and more agile than I am even now that I'm free of my suit. Though they have little chance of hurting me, they can keep me pinned down, and I don't like to think of what might happen to Tamara if I don't catch up quickly.

I need a weapon. On instinct, I reach out and catch one of the missiles, lobbing it back at the nearest humanoid.

My attackers cease firing, and surprise and respect flash against my *Iki'i*. Their attention drops to my erection, which I only now realize is still in place. I widen my stance, keeping my hips thrust forward to show it off. "Let me pass."

A humanoid with a broad chest holds out one of the yellow projectiles, then makes a motion to the surrounding trees. "Va Sheeghr tribe?"

It takes me a moment, but then I realize they're asking if I'm from another tribe. I look nothing like them, but perhaps there are other species roaming this planet. "I'm Kirenai," I say.

The broad-chested humanoid gestures to the forest again. "More?"

It might be helpful if these humanoids know I'm not alone. "Yes. More. Many more."

A smaller Sheeghr purrs, "Fffemales?"

Uh, oh. I don't want these horny locals hunting for female passengers. To be fair, there are no female Kirenai, so I shake my head, grab my cock with one hand, and point down the path. "My female."

A heartbeat passes. Another. Then the broad-chested one points toward the trail. "Come."

The other two growl and shift their weight, as if unsure about this decision, but then return to the trail and retrieve the pole bearing the carcass of something black and segmented suspended by rope mesh. At least it doesn't appear to be another passenger from the shuttle.

As they start off down the trail, I hurry over and pick up my flight suit. I consider putting it back on, then think better of it. If I need to wave my dick around again, it will be better to have it out already. I stuff my suit into Tamara's bag and loop the strap around my neck.

The humanoids are already disappearing into the brush, so with a last glance over the wreckage, I set off after them. I hope the other passengers can find each other on their own and don't run into any more trouble.

10

TAZHIO

The humanoids lead me with unerring confidence over the tangled roots. Little to no sunlight reaches this deep into the forest, but my guides move easily through shadows and glowing vegetation alike. It takes longer than I like to catch up to the pair carrying Tamara, who are obviously unhappy to see me with their friends. The group snarls and chitters, cocks raised like masts among them. I originally thought the word Sheeghr meant cock, but it turns out it's the name these people call themselves.

"Tazhio, what's going on?" Tamara asks hoarsely, swinging from her bound hands and feet on the pole as the Sheeghr gesture wildly and chatter over one another in excitement. "Can you understand them?"

"A little. My translator is still learning." They're obviously in dispute about whether to take me with them, but I don't have a context for much of their reasoning.

Suddenly, the leader hands his end of Tamara's pole to another and shoves his muzzle close to my face. His breath smells like river water as he growls, "Toozeer gary."

The two Sheeghr carrying Tamara move a few steps into the brush, as if preparing to run off again.

"Wait!" I don't know what a toozeer gary is, but I doubt Tamara will enjoy whatever it is. I can't stop them from taking her, but hell if I'll let her go face this alone. Willing my cock to grow larger, I broaden my chest and shoulders for good measure. "I will come, too. Untie the female and let me carry her."

The leader stares at me a moment, then heaves a sigh and pulls a crude knife from his belt. In a couple of swift strokes, he's severed Tamara's bindings. She lands on the ground with a thud, rolling onto her side and rubbing her wrists. The leaf I bound over the scratch in her leg is askew, and a crimson trail of blood marks her pale ankle.

The tall Sheeghr nudges me from behind. "You gary. Go."

Ah, gary means carry. That makes more sense. Perhaps Toozeer is their leader. "They want me to carry you. Okay?"

She nods and I slide my arms under her knees and shoulders, cradling her to my chest. My erection tingles with awareness of her nearness as we walk.

"Do you know where they're taking us?" Her voice sounds choked, and she's trembling violently.

I hold her tighter. "No. But wherever we end up, I won't let them hurt you."

Her arms tighten around my neck. "Thank you."

As I follow the Sheeghr deeper into the forest, I pray I can keep my promise.

11

TAMARA

I'm nearly numb from anxiety overload as I cling to Tazhio's neck and focus on simply breathing for a few minutes. Every time I think my panic has reached a new threshold, something else happens. I need my dog. I want to go home. Hell, even some salve for the rope burns on my wrists and ankles would be nice. It takes everything I have to keep myself present in the here and now instead of turning into a catatonic zombie.

You're alive, I keep repeating to myself until the words have no meaning, so I switch to focusing on the warmth of Tazhio's powerful arms and chest as we follow the ferret aliens deeper into the trees. I'm not certain if they intended to rape me or have me for dinner—or both, but at least Tazhio has stopped them for now.

My mind is still spinning over the accident, though, and I need answers. I touch the strap of my bag hanging from Tazhio's shoulder. "Did you find Beanie? I thought I heard him barking."

He nods. "He's alive, but refused to come to me."

A small sob of relief fills my chest. "And my sisters? The other passengers? What happened to them?"

"I didn't have a chance to find them, but the safety restraints should've protected everyone." He grimaces. "The problem is that they're scattered all over the forest."

My heart constricts, and I look at the ferret alien walking in front of us. He's carrying one end of the centipede carcass and rocks back and forth as he walks, as if he's unaccustomed to using only two legs. But I still remember how fast they moved on four legs, and how easily they took down that centipede monster. Then there was the way they responded to me...

I gulp, imagining my sisters encountering these creatures. "What if these ferret aliens find them?"

Tazhio's lips are a hard line, and he keeps his attention on the aliens ahead. "One thing at a time, *kikajiru*. Let's figure out what they want first."

One alien growls something, and several others make a chittering sound that might be laughter. I'm once again filled with dread about where we might be going and why.

"Are they taking us to their village?"

Tazhio tilts his head, listening to them chitter and purr. "That would make sense. They likely have a settlement somewhere nearby."

"Why are they insisting we go with them?"

"I think they want us to meet their leader."

"That makes sense, I suppose." I rest my cheek against his bare shoulder, breathing in his masculine scent layered with a hint of what I can only define as tropical. "Thank you for coming to my rescue." My voice thickens as I recall those terrifying moments when the ferret aliens came toward me. "I dread thinking of what they wanted to do to me."

"Don't worry." His arms squeeze me gently. "I won't let them touch you."

He steps over a bump in the path, and the head of his cock nudges my ass. I try to ignore it because I'm pretty sure he just competed in some sort of dick-measuring contest on my behalf, and he probably needs time to let his hard-on wear off. But my panties grow damp, and I can't help squeezing my thighs together at the memory of his impressive size. Are all the blue aliens that big? Seems there should've been a warning in the dating brochure. *Or a selling point.*

I push back those thoughts. I should be coming up with a plan to get away from these ferret creatures, not thinking about riding a big blue dick. But it's hard to focus on anything else when I'm skin-to-skin with a powerful, naked man.

Seeming to sense my discomfort, Tazhio clears his throat. "I hope my earlier display did not offend you. The Sheeghr determine rank by the size of one's phallus." As if to reinforce his point, his cock brushes my ass again. *How long can he stay hard?* "I must compete for respect."

Heat floods my cheeks as I imagine uses other than competition for status. I swallow thickly. "Well, keep up the good work."

A smile twitches the corners of his lips. "I'll keep it up as long as it takes."

The heat in my cheeks intensifies, and I choke back a giggle. *Good Lord, how can we be flirting at a time like this?* But it feels good to get my mind off our current situation.

Ahead, the ferret aliens stop without warning, and Tazhio's smile twists back to a frown. The tallest one chitters quietly, and I think I hear the word danger repeated. Is it possible I'm learning their language? Maybe my universal translator thing will come in handy after all.

"What is it?" I ask.

Gaze scanning the area, Tazhio answers, "I believe they detect a predator ahead."

One ferret turns and hisses at us.

"He's asking for silence," Tazhio whispers.

My arms tighten around his neck as we continue forward, slogging off the trail to tiptoe around something that looks like a Venus flytrap with alligator heads. Several enormous mouths are open to expose gleaming, leaf-like teeth, and one closed mouth holds something the size of a large dog that twitches and jerks. *God, I hope Beanie's okay.* He wouldn't stand a chance against monsters like that. I need to get back and find him.

My heartbeat doesn't stop racing until we're well past the spot and the ferrets resume their purring chatter. I can swear I'm now catching words here and there. Home. Food. Danger.

Still keeping to a whisper, I ask, "Will my translator learn their language eventually, too?"

"Yes, but mine will learn faster because of my *Iki'i,*" Tazhio replies, his voice also still soft.

I'm about to ask what an *Iki'i* is when I spot another group of ferret aliens approaching on all fours through the murky green light. There are at least a dozen, scurrying, chittering, purring, tussling. Several of our escorts call out, and I hold my breath as the newcomers near. Am I about to witness another dick jousting contest? But although the new ferrets circle us curiously, they make no sexual display and don't appear to be aggressive.

"They are young ones, I believe," says Tazhio, never breaking stride as the new ferret aliens keep pace by leap-frogging over each other beside the trail. Some run ahead, while some fall to wrestling and drop behind.

Soon we reach a small creek trickling between the roots and turn to follow it. Ahead, the trees open onto a clearing where the ground terraces up in a long slope to the base of a gargantuan tree trunk, the largest I've ever seen. A hollow in its broad side forms a cavern with golden yellow light radiating from inside. Emerging from the mouth is a horde of ferret aliens.

And it looks as if every one of them has his dick out.

12

TAZHIO

 $\mathcal{M}$ y steps slow at the sight of the oncoming group of Sheeghr. There are too many to count, and unlike the young ones who followed along with us earlier, it seems as if every one of these Sheeghr sports a bright pink erection.

"Oh, God," Tamara gasps, body rigid in my arms.

The horde races to surround us, pushing and wriggling to get a glimpse of the newcomers as we follow the burbling stream up toward the cavern. We climb terraces filled with cultivated rows of plants, and several of the Sheeghr standing between the rows hold what I assume are agricultural tools. I'm worried they'll be turned into weapons if the situation goes bad, and clutch Tamara firmly against my chest, lifting her higher to allow my cock to show prominently. How far can my display get me among so many competitors? The Sheeghr traveling with us from the crash site hadn't hesitated to start violence with their slingshots. I can't let this escalate into a bloodbath—especially with Tamara as the prize.

"Fffertile." The word is repeated among the crowd, and my *Iki'i* is drowning in a single emotion—*lust*. I'm forced to shut down my senses before I'm overwhelmed by the bombardment of prurience.

"The female is mine." I bare my teeth at any Sheeghr who comes too close.

"Why are they so interested in me?" Tamara's voice shakes. "Don't they have any women of their own?"

I've been wondering the same thing; so far I haven't seen a single adult individual without a phallus on display. "I don't know." I stare down a Sheeghr with bushy black eyebrows who is hovering too close for comfort. "But I won't let them touch you."

Tamara cringes away from a particularly energetic member of the crowd who is stroking himself with lewd abandon. "There are so many. How can you stop them?"

"Let me worry about that," I say, keeping my voice calmer than I feel.

Ahead, the roiling crowd parts in a wave, revealing an overly large Sheeghr with dark purple fur and huge glittering eyes. In one six-fingered hand it clutches a gnarled staff inset with pink crystals, and its stomach is distended and heavy. *Pregnant.*

In the cave's mouth behind her, more Sheeghr stand waiting, not a dick in sight, and I realize we've just discovered where they keep their females.

"Look. They do have women." I smile reassuringly.

Tamara sighs. "Oh, thank God."

The males escorting us drop the segmented carcass they're carrying at the female's feet. The tallest of their captors points toward Tamara. "This fertile one is offended. We brought her here to be soothed so she might evolve."

My translator struggles with the nuances of the words while the crowd boils with excitement, hips gyrating and phalluses throbbing. A spurt of what might be ejaculate carves an arc through the air and lands at my feet. I bare my teeth and search the nearby crowd for the culprit.

"Take her, take her," a few in the crowd begin to chant.

"My female," I roar.

The crowd backs up, but their chittering grows higher pitched, anger beating against my shuttered *Iki'i*.

The pregnant female thumps the base of her staff against the ground, and the crowd quiets. "Females choose." She stands almost a head higher than any of the other Sheeghr and emanates a sense of command. "Not males."

This might be good news for Tamara, but I need to be sure I understand correctly. Focusing on the leader, I open my *Iki'i* a crack, wincing at the heightened emotions that immediately zing across my senses. I grit my teeth and endure. I need every advantage if we hope to establish an understanding with these people.

"What's she saying?" Tamara asks.

"She says females choose, not males."

"Really?" Tamara pats my chest with one hand, a steely resolve emerging from her nebula of fear. "Then let me stand."

Surprised, I lower her gently to her feet but keep one arm around her waist for support if she needs it.

Facing the female with the staff, Tamara points at me with her free hand and speaks slowly, "I choose him."

The pregnant female turns a critical eye toward me. Her gaze drops to my crotch, and I push my hips forward as I've seen so many of her males do. But I sense only disdain as she returns her gaze to Tamara. "I am called Zeer from the Dovlu matrilineal line. What are you called, female?"

Tamara grimaces and glances at me. "My translator didn't catch any of that. What did she say?"

"She says her name is Zeer and asks for yours." I'm not used to being dismissed, but I'm wary about what is culturally acceptable here. The knots on the leader's staff resemble female labias, each crystal embedded in the swollen slits made to look like a pink bud of pleasure, and I'm beginning to think that the females rule. It's good Tamara is stepping up to speak for herself, and I hope my need to translate won't count against her.

Straightening her shoulders, Tamara stares down the Sheeghr leader, outwardly confident, even though her anxiety rails against my senses. "My name's Tamara. This male I've chosen is Tazhio. I insist you let us go now."

Zeer stares pointedly at my dick. "I have not seen a mating rod this color. Is that why it is defective?"

The crowd chortles.

Tamara flushes and looks sideways at my crotch.

Just her glance makes me grow painfully hard, and I push more of my matrix into the shaft, swelling it further. What is the Sheeghr female trying to accomplish by belittling me? I obviously dwarf every one of these other males in size. Thrusting my hips forward, I say, "I am more than adequate."

The surrounding Sheeghr erupt into a chittering discussion peppered by both admiration and doubt. "Impregnate."

"Fertile."

"Insufficient."

That steely sensation coming from Tamara grows more solid, and to my utter surprise, she reaches over and grips my engorged shaft.

Kuzara! Excruciating bliss makes my eyes flutter briefly as all my earlier fantasies about her crowd my mind. I'm filled with a single thought. *Mine.* My arm at her waist flexes, pulling her tightly against my side. This is not the time or place to lose control. Yet all it will take is one firm stroke of her palm and I'll spill my seed all over the ground.

"My male is strong," Tamara says, baring her teeth toward the Sheeghr female, her small hand still firmly around my girth. Her translator might not be picking up the language yet, but she obviously has the gist of the situation.

I breathe shallowly, unable to think straight, let alone speak.

Zeer blinks, radiating confusion. "Then why are you not with child?"

Gathering what I can of my wits, I shift my attention to the females assembled at the mouth of the cave.

Most are visibly pregnant, and I have a feeling the rest probably are also, just not yet showing.

"What did she say?" asks Tamara from the corner of her mouth.

"She asks why you're not pregnant." My voice is thick in my throat. Does she have any idea what her touch is doing to me?

Tamara sucks in a breath, and her hand leaves my dick. "Are you kidding me?"

Losing the pressure of her hand around my shaft is almost painful, and I take a steadying breath. I'm not sure there's enough blood in my head right now to interpret anything correctly. "Look at how many of them are pregnant."

She turns her head to scan the females assembled at the cave mouth. Just then, the tall male who captured us pipes up, "They said there are more males in the forest, plenty to fill this female, yet she remains empty."

Zeer's six-fingered hand slides down her staff, bumping over the knots along its length almost suggestively. "Perhaps she requires an Orgy of Alignment."

I take a beat to let my translator sift through the words. But the reignited lust pounding against my *Iki'i* forces a single word from between my teeth as I glare at the crowd. "Mine."

They chitter louder, and Zeer scowls. "Let the female speak."

We need to stop things before they go any further, but Tamara doesn't yet have an adequate grasp of their language. I hold up both hands in a sign of peace. "She doesn't understand your language. We are visitors from far away, only here by accident. Our females often go a long time without breeding. Please allow us to be on our way."

The crowd rustles, filling the air with disbelief and no small amount of worry.

"Impossible." Zeer points the top of her staff toward Tamara. "Females who do not breed are dangerous."

"No. Our females are not like Sheeghr. We are different." I point to my erection, which Zeer had already commented on as unusual.

Zeer pounds her staff. "Unmated females attract Gloor. If this female can't or won't take a male's seed, she must be removed."

The crowd shifts like a tide, murmuring, "Menace."

"Blood."

"Slaughter."

Tamara is trembling against my side, head moving from side to side frantically as she looks at the Sheeghr. "What are they saying?"

I don't want to frighten her more than she already is, but I can't deny that my own panic is rising by the second. "They fear something called a Gloor. They think you're going to attract it." Taking a deep breath, I address Zeer. "What is this creature you speak of?"

Zeer shakes her head. "Not a creature. Gloor is the Twisted God. He comes at night seeking unmated females to carry his eggs. His progeny are ravenous and will consume everyone in the village."

The crowd grows more agitated as Zeer explains, and several now raise blades as well as voices.

"Just let us go," I say. "We'll go far from the village and trouble you no more."

"No." Zeer raises her voice over the roiling crowd. "She will take a male's seed this night, or tomorrow she must die."

"Jesus!" Tamara makes a choking sound. "Did she just say I have to fuck them or die?"

My mind is only half on my answer as I search the area for anything to help us escape. "I don't think it's a matter of sex so much as pregnancy."

"Hell no!" Balling her hands into fists, Tamara plants her back against me as if ready to face them all down. "I'm not getting pregnant with some alien ferret baby."

The crowd is too close, and there is nowhere for us to go, nothing to serve as a distraction. I could envelop her in my matrix to keep them from touching her, but that won't last more than a few minutes if the Sheeghr use their toxin on me. I don't know what to do. All I can think is that I've failed her.

"Prepare her for the Orgy of Alignment!" shouts Zeer.

Several Sheeghr move toward us with ropes. I slug the nearest in the muzzle, knocking him back.

Another grabs my arm, while a third throws a net over my head. Tamara screams as a second net pulls her to the ground. I break free of one Sheeghr's grip, but more hands pin me down. Within moments, we're both bound, and Tamara is being hauled inside the cave.

"Tamara!" I shout. I've lost sight of her, though I can still hear her screams, and it's killing me.

Zeer comes to stand over me. After a moment of watching my useless struggles, she lowers the tip of her staff and presses it against my chest. "You are not of our ways, but she chose you. If you agree to abide, I will offer you the honor of first penetration."

I stop struggling against the ropes. From the moment we met, I dreamed of being with her. I know she wants me, too. I've sensed it many times, even as recently as our trek through the forest. But I know if I try to impregnate her, it will turn into more. I want to make her my mate. To form a permanent bond. I won't be able to stop myself. My desire for her is too strong.

I feel sick to my stomach. She shouldn't be forced to choose between me and the Sheeghr, but there are no other options.

With a sigh, I tell Zeer, "There will be no need for an orgy. I accept your offer."

Zeer raises her wispy purple eyebrows. "Good." She gestures to the Sheeghr who are restraining me. "Present him to the female. But if she refuses, we will prepare the Orgy."

TAMARA

his is not happening. They've tossed me into a circular enclosure in the back of the enormous tree cavern, and dozens of ferret-like Sheeghr now leer at me through the wooden bars, penises still grotesquely engorged. I'm having a nightmare, right? Any moment I'll wake up in my own bed, soaked in sweat and shaking, but Beanie will be licking my face and telling me it will all be okay. *Beanie, where are you?*

After a minute of lying there trying to calm my racing heart, I have to accept I'm not dreaming. This is all too real. From the prickle of the dead leaves I'm lying on to the strange, half-intelligible mutterings from the ferret aliens on the other side of the bars. I feel like a hamster in a cage, and all I want to do is burrow down into the litter and hide.

Instead, I force myself to inhale a shivering breath. Freezing with panic won't help. I need to remain calm and think. I stare at the high ceiling. It's plastered with bright yellow and fuchsia plants. My therapist suggested focusing on the positive when I feel stressed, but I can't come up with many positive thoughts right now, so instead I imagine the pattern of plants overhead is a cross-stitch project. I count the stitches until I'm no longer gasping for air.

Slowly, I sit up. The horrid aliens are still packed around my cage, but beyond them I see that the cavern floor is terraced like the ground was outside. A cascade of water gushes from a crack in the cavern's wood wall and flows in a steady stream past my prison toward the exit. The burbling stream can't block out the muttering crowd, and my translator keeps picking up on key words like fuck and death. A tiny crack opens in my numbness, and I realize I'm angry. Not angry - *furious*. These creeps want to turn me into a sex slave.

Balling my hands into fists until my nails bite into my palms, I glare through the bars at a nearby ferret who has big dark eyes that make him look a bit less feral than the others. Then he grins, showing blunt gray teeth and waggles his erection at me. Okay, maybe I was wrong about him seeming less feral. He dips a cup into the stream and thrusts it between the bars. "Choose me."

I bat the cup away with a hiss, spilling water across the leaves. "I don't want you and I don't want water. I want out. Where's Tazhio?" They didn't bring him to the cage with me, so where is he? Is he hurt? My throat tightens. *What if they killed him?*

Another alien shoves a bowl of gray mush that smells like dirty feet into the cage. "Good. Pleasure."

Bile rises into my throat, and I scoot backward until my spine hits the cavern wall. Last time I threw up, they hog-tied me and carried me away, and I don't want to find out what they'll do to me if I vomit again.

A ferret alien with brilliant, almost magenta-colored stripes smooths a six-fingered hand over the fur on his chest and purrs, "Me. Protect. Gloor."

"If you're so worried I'm going to attract this Gloor thing, then why did you bring me to your village? Let me go and I'll lure it away." I stand up, realizing this might be exactly the argument they need to hear.

But my admirers turn away as a mummy-looking figure appears over the heads of the crowd. It's being passed along from hand to hand, and when it reaches the bars, the crowd surges forward and dumps it over the top into my enclosure. The mummy plops to the floor, looking like it's been flattened by a mac truck. Between the thick rope bindings, I see patches of familiar blue skin.

"Tazhio!" Terrified they've killed him, I rush over to check, falling to my knees beside him.

He sits up and shakes off the ropes, his limbs rippling and reforming like liquid. I halt with my hand outstretched. This is the first time I've seen a Kirenai alter his shape, and it's incredible. Outside the bars, the ferret aliens are also chittering exclamations of awe.

I sit back on my knees, feeling like my eyes are going to bug out of my head. "Are you okay?"

"I'm fine. There's little they can do to hurt me." He looks me over as though checking for injuries. Then he lifts the leaf bandage on my leg, revealing a long scab. "What about you?"

I'd almost forgotten about the scratch, but moving the bandage still makes me wince. "I'm okay, but—"

A loud banging sound cuts me off. I turn to see the pregnant female called Zeer knocking her staff against the bars. "If fertility later exists," the Sheeghr leader announces over the noise of the chortling crowd, "Orgy of Alignment begins."

Shit. It sounds like the gang rape is moving forward. I lift my chin defiantly. "I won't go down without a fight. Rape is a crime among my people."

"Rape?" Zeer cocks her head. "Word not known."

"Force me to have sex."

Zeer stiffens as if offended. "Force not! Female to choose."

"I already chose Tazhio! Why did you lock us up?"

The Sheeghr leader responds with a rap of her staff against the bars. "Safe space for you to ensure fertility."

The pit of my stomach flip-flops as I realize they're expecting me to have sex with Tazhio right here, right now. While they watch. Still, I turn to him for verification. "What's she saying?"

Tazhio folds the leaf bandage and tosses it aside before meeting my gaze. "You chose me, and…" He swallows, and his eyes dart to the onlooking crowd before he continues. "And they've agreed to allow you to have sex with me first."

"First?" I choke out, staring out the bars toward the glistening pink palisade of ferret alien erections.

"Don't panic," he says, reaching toward me, then pausing as if unsure. "If you get pregnant right away, none of them will touch you."

I can't help the hysterical laugh that escapes my throat. "Getting pregnant can take months! Besides, I don't want to have a baby. Not yet, at least."

His lips press into a hard line. "It may actually be a blessing they found us. If I understand them correctly, there's a creature or a parasite on this planet that they believe is a god. It lays its eggs in fertile women, and when the eggs hatch, the brood eats the woman and apparently everyone else nearby. The Sheeghr keep their females continually pregnant to prevent that from happening."

"Oh, God." I gasp in horror, wrapping my arms around my chest. "Is that what this Gloor thing is?" I've seen a few nature shows where wasps lay eggs in other insects, followed by horrifying sped-up images of the babies eating the host alive. My insides squirm at the idea, and I feel like I can't breathe. To think I just offered to lure it away from the village... "You mean they're trying to protect me?"

"I guess so, yes."

Then I go back to the other issue. Sex. Tazhio is offering to have sex with me. I recall his massive erection, and heat floods my entire body as my attention shifts to his lap. I can tell he's still hard even though leaves and rope cover his lap. Swallowing thickly, I say, "I'm not on birth control, but most people don't get pregnant the first time."

He puts his fingertips gently on my knee. "Humans have proven to be highly receptive to Kirenai mating. I have no worry about your ability to carry my child."

A zing of arousal races through me, and the flutters in my stomach move downward to my pelvis, settling with low heat between my legs. I lift my gaze to his face. The same desire I remember seeing in the elevator is there, and I bite my lip, recalling the way his mouth had felt on mine.

I quickly drop my attention back to the contrast of his blue skin against my pale knee. My mouth has gone completely dry, and my lungs feel like they're being squeezed by a giant hand. I'm super conscious of the ferret aliens still watching us outside the cage, and I don't think my introverted heart can feature in a porno show for them without exploding. "Are they planning to watch… everything we do?"

Tazhio sighs. "Yes." He takes my hand, squeezing my fingers gently. "But there's something else I need you to understand. I can't make love to you without forming a bond."

I frown. Why is he warning me about something like that? A man who forms an attachment during sex is more than I could ever hope for, especially in a situation like this. Perhaps aliens think that's weird. His expression is so serious, I feel I have to ask, "Is that… bad?"

His dark eyes are like bottomless pools as he gazes into my face. I have his total attention as he says, "Kirenai mate for life."

My heart is beating so fast, I think he must be able to hear it pounding against my ribs. *A mate for life.* No worries about being ditched for someone else. No deadbeat dad. No concern about growing old alone. And Tazhio is not only sexy as hell, he's proven to be a caring, protective man.

But then I realize Tazhio is actually saying this isn't about me. It's about *him*. I'm not the only one who'll be locked into the bond. He's offering to give up all hope of future relationships just to save my life. *Well, fuck.* I can't ask him to do that, no matter how much I want to avoid those disgusting ferret things.

I firmly remove my fingers from his grip. "I can't."

14

TAZHIO

*T*amara's sudden rejection takes me off guard. She'd prefer to lie with one of the Sheeghr over bonding with me? I'd been using my *Iki'i* to gauge Tamara's emotions, and I never once detected her attraction to one of these males. I lean forward, frowning as I try to understand. "Am I so terrible a fate?"

"It's not you!" A pretty pink flush blooms over her freckled cheeks, but she refuses to meet my gaze. "I just don't expect you to ruin your life to save mine."

"Ruin my...?" Then I understand what she's implying. She thinks I'm offering this out of pity. I take her hand again, caressing the back of her knuckles with my thumb. "You have the wrong idea.

I've dreamed of bonding with you since the moment we met."

"You're just saying that to make me feel better." She attempts to pull her hand free, but I hold it firmly.

"Even if I am, that doesn't mean it's not true."

Her gray eyes are stormy. "Then why didn't you come with me after the party? You led me on with a kiss, then abandoned me when the elevator reached my floor."

Now I understand. She thought I rejected her. That I hadn't wanted to be with her, even though the opposite was true. "I'm sorry. I certainly didn't mean to hurt your feelings. It's just that they forbid the crew from socializing with the female guests." Her doubt feels like a wall of thorns against my *Iki'i*, and her lips are pressed into a tight line, but I continue anyway. "But those rules no longer apply now that we're stuck down here."

She finally raises her gaze to mine, her eyebrows furrowed with confusion. "But we're not talking about having a fling. We're talking about bonding or mating or whatever and having a child. We hardly even know each other."

"I never wanted to have a fling, Tamara. You will make an excellent mate and mother. I'll be honored to claim you as mine."

"You think I will, huh? Tell me, then." She lifts her chin in challenge. "What, exactly, do you like about me?"

She thinks I can't come up with anything, when the real problem is that I'm attracted to everything about her. I don't know where to start. "The first moment I saw you, I was drawn to your hair." I reach out with my free hand and push a copper curl behind her ear. "It's a bit like a Fogarian's, but much prettier."

"Pfft." She remains stiff, doubt still stinging my *Iki'i*. "There were at least a dozen women on that ship with reddish hair, my sisters included, and every one of them is way more attractive than I am. Plus, the color of my hair says nothing about me as a person."

I frown. I don't like to hear her talk that way about herself. "You are amazing. I can tell you are nurturing because of the way you care for your dog. I love how brave you are—"

"Ha!" she interrupts. "Brave? I've been quaking in my boots since the moment I spotted the shuttle on the tarmac."

"Yet you got on board anyway. That's brave."

She stares at me as if stunned, a flush rising up her throat and spreading across her cheeks. "No one's ever called me that before."

I drop my voice, leaning forward to speak more intimately with her. "It's true. And I think you're the sexiest woman on the *Romantasy*. I had to pleasure myself every time I thought about you." Her eyes widen in shock, but her arousal floods my *Iki'i*. I grin. "Which happened a *lot*."

"Oh." The pinkness in her cheeks deepens to red.

I can no longer resist. I press my mouth against hers. For a single heartbeat, she remains rigid, then softens, opening to me.

I sweep my tongue past her teeth into her sweet mouth. She's as exquisite as I imagined, hot and breathy and willing. Her arms wrap around my neck, her tongue dancing with mine. I thread my fingers into the hair at the nape of her neck, deepening the kiss. She hasn't said yes, but she hasn't outright told me no, either.

She moans softly into my mouth. *Kuzara*, she's enough to drive a man crazy.

I palm one of her breasts. Through the fabric of her blouse, her nipple hardens to a peak. I'm dying to touch her skin, to explore every inch of her with my hands and my mouth. I push her gently back against the leafy ground, my lips still locked on hers. The Sheeghr are muttering approval, and I'm worried it will become a distraction, so I hum a low growl to drown them out.

As I hoped, she seems to find the sound attractive, and her fingers creep around my shoulders, fingers threading my hair. I can sense she's nervous, but her desire for me is primary, and I love it.

I slide my palm down to her waist and up under her shirt, skimming her softness. She wears another layer over her breasts, something with a wire and what feels like lace. I growl low in my throat at the barrier and tease her hardened nipple through the fabric.

She gasps and arches up to meet me.

I nudge one knee between her legs, pressing my thigh up to her apex. My dick is a rod of agony, waiting to be quenched. Feathering my mouth along her jaw to her ear, I murmur, "I don't know how to remove your clothes."

She nods mutely, panting as I push my knee against her center in a pulsing rhythm, my hand alternately kneading her breast and circling her nipple. Twisting one arm around behind her, she releases a clasp, and the underclothing pops loose around her ribs.

I nip her earlobe as I slide my fingers under the wire. Her full softness fills my palm, and I groan with pleasure. Her skin is warm and velvety soft, the nipple puckered to a tight bud, and I no longer have patience for mere teasing. I thrust her blouse up to expose her to me and lower my mouth to her flesh. I suck the nipple in, hard, then release it and roll my tongue around the point, nipping and sucking until she's mewling like a newborn *nezumi*.

"Delectable," I murmur, lips still against her skin.

Her hips are rocking against my leg, and my cock is harder than it's ever been, surging with desire every time her hip rubs against my balls. "Your pants," I growl, and begin kissing my way down her belly.

She doesn't hesitate. With one hand, she yanks the drawstring loose and pushes the waistband down to expose the lacy top of her panties.

I have no patience for any further barriers and yank the garment off her legs, grudging that I have to break away from her heat to do it. Through the lace of her panties, I spy the dark copper curls covering her sex. My dick throbs at the sight. I want to rip the fragile cloth aside and bury my face between her legs, but I know this may be the only clothing she has for a very long time, so I slowly hook a finger beneath the band and ease it away from her mound. The scent of her arousal reaches me, warm and musky. None of my self-pleasuring imagination can compare with the real thing.

Lowering myself once more to her belly, I kiss the tender skin just above her pubic bone as I pull the panties down her hips. When the thin fabric reaches her knees, she lifts one leg and pulls her foot free. The parting of her thighs calls to me, and I put my palms against her soft skin, holding them open. I lower my mouth to her slit, sliding my tongue along it over the swollen nub barely poking from between her lower lips.

She cries out, legs going stiff in surprise. But I also feel the zing of her delight, the cresting desire inside her.

I lick her again, flattening my tongue and applying more pressure until she parts like a flower, releasing the delicacy of her arousal. She's slick and hot, and I plunge my tongue deeply into her channel while my hands hold her thighs apart.

Her inner walls flutter, and she moans loudly. I block out the chittering sounds of the Sheeghr watching us, glad Tamara seems blissfully lost to her own pleasure as I continue stroking, rubbing my tongue over a ridged spot that seems to please her. I push deeper while my dick throbs with the need to feel her around me. *Patience.* I will bring her to ecstasy over and over before we are through.

I move up again to circle my tongue over her clit. It's engorged and pulsing. She's breathing hard, both hands clutched loosely in my hair. My cock is throbbing with anticipation as I crawl back up her body and position it at her entrance. I rub the swollen head between her wet folds, and she flexes up to meet me, legs widening and breath speeding up. "Take me," she pants.

I thrust forward, burying myself to the hilt in her pulsing heat.

She inhales sharply and stiffens.

I pause, suddenly worried. "Did I hurt you?"

Eyes squeezed shut, she shakes her head. "You're big."

My *Iki'i* senses that she doesn't mind the slight pain —enjoys it, even—nevertheless, I offer, "I can make myself smaller."

Her eyes fly open, a small crease between her eyebrows. "No!"

A triumphant growl rises in my throat. I pull back and thrust deep into her slippery heat. My eyes roll back at the rapturous sensation of her tightness. If I'm not careful, I'll spill myself inside her before she orgasms again, and I want more than ever to feel her come around me. "*Kuzara*," I grit out, grasping at every ounce of control as I repeat the pull and push, pausing deep inside her each time so the organ at the top of my shaft can stimulate her clit.

She gasps, arching up to meet my strokes, her skin glistening with a slight sheen of perspiration that slicks between us as I increase my pace. Each stroke is pure madness, and coupled with the lustful emotions pounding the edges of my *Iki'i* from the surrounding Sheeghr, I don't know how I'm going to keep myself from exploding before she reaches her climax.

My secondary mating shaft is throbbing with the need to penetrate her backside, to insert the genetic marker that will claim her as my mate, and it takes every ounce of my willpower to hold back. I can impregnate her without claiming her, but I don't want to. I want my life bound to hers in every way possible.

Her body begins to shake with a rising orgasm, and I pound her harder, faster, driving her over the edge until she cries out in pleasure.

No longer able to restrain myself, I extrude my mating shaft. It probes her ass, sliding through the juices flowing between us and easing into her puckered hole before her orgasm has completed. The double sensation makes me groan, and I open my eyes to see her gaping at me, mouth open in surprise even as her body continues to spasm.

"Tazhio," she chokes out, pupils wells of dark desire. Her hands claw into my back as though she's holding on for dear life. "Oh, God!"

"I will cherish you for the rest of my life, Tamara," I growl. Then I slam myself home once, twice, three times before ejaculating my seed deep inside her womb. Never did I imagine the pleasure of sex could be so consuming. So spiritually life altering. I see stars. Planets. Entire solar systems spread out before me.

I bury my face against the side of her throat, panting. "You are mine."

15

TAMARA

The heat of Tazhio's cum pumping into me draws my orgasm to incredible heights; I think I must be having an out-of-body experience from the pleasure. By the time I feel like I can breathe again, my arms and legs feel like jelly and my entire body tingles with a warm glow of satisfaction. He's collapsed on top of me, panting against my neck. I take a moment to recognize that the chittering I'm hearing is from the ferret aliens still watching us outside the cage. I resist the urge to look at them, not ready to lose the sliver of intimacy I'm feeling at the moment.

Tazhio lifts his head to look into my eyes. "Did you find pleasure in our bonding?"

I'm still spent from our activities, or I'm sure I would laugh at his question. Instead, I say, "Are you kidding? That was amazing."

He gives me a lazy smile that makes me feel all fuzzy. "We're mated now."

I swallow. "Are you sure? I don't feel any different."

"Of course you don't feel different." He gives me a self-satisfied wink. "You've loved me from the moment we met."

"Cocky bastard." But I can't help grinning. He's right, of course.

Then my throat tightens as I think about the second part of our coupling. *Am I pregnant now?* How would the ferret aliens even know? I let myself glance at the Sheeghr milling around outside the bars. It looks as if they're having an orgy of their own now. Couples rut gleefully on the floor, and solitary males watch while stroking themselves. At least they appear to have lost interest in us. "When do you think they'll let us go?"

Tazhio rolls aside, pulling me with him to lie on his chest. He kisses my forehead. "Once they can verify you're pregnant. I'm guessing their senses can detect it very early since it's so important to their survival."

A tight ball of worry remains in my stomach, a dichotomy of emotions at the thought of having a baby versus the concern that I can't. I have several friends who had trouble conceiving, and one who gave up. I try not to think about what will happen if Tazhio doesn't get me pregnant. My sister, Suzanne, got knocked up with twins at seventeen, so I hope fertility runs in our family.

I fall asleep in Tazhio's arms, and when I wake, the light in the cavern hasn't changed. As I stretch, I idly wonder if the plants ever go dark. My shirt and shorts are draped over me along with my bag, which immediately makes me long for Beanie. I pray he's alive and well and reunited with my sisters and the other passengers. Sitting up, I feel like a homeless person sleeping under a bunch of newspapers, but I'm grateful my nakedness isn't on full display.

Then I realize Tazhio's nowhere in sight. My heart kicks into overdrive and I look around frantically. Four ferret aliens guard the enclosure, each holding a spear and looking outward, as if protecting me from someone coming in rather than me getting out.

I quickly pull my clothing back on, watching the activity on the terraces outside the cage. The community seems to have returned to daily life, cooking and weaving and whatever other mundane tasks need tending. It's as if having someone locked in a cage in their midst is an everyday occurrence. I think longingly of the water I batted away when I first arrived. My throat is parched, and the stream is just out of reach of the cage. But I hesitate to engage with the guards for fear they'll try to molest me again. I much prefer they continue facing away from me.

Then I see a familiar blue figure striding between the groups of Sheeghr toward the cage. My heart swells with relief. Tazhio's carrying a netted bag in one hand and a tall, thin jug in the other. When he reaches the bars, his body thins, and he slips between the slats, easily resuming his normal shape once inside. I shake my head, still in awe of this ability.

He holds out the bag. "I gathered some food and water."

Remembering the bowl of porridge one of the Sheeghr offered me earlier, I wrinkle my nose. The bag holds what looks like golf ball-sized purple fruits, long white sticks, and some wrinkled brown items that might be nuts. "What are those?"

"Food. The Sheeghr shared with me. I've sampled these items, but you should start by trying just one and see if it agrees with you. I suggest the *urru*." He sits cross-legged on the ground and removes one of the golf balls. With a twist, it comes apart to reveal a juicy, nearly black interior. He holds half out to me. "Here."

I can't deny the pinch of hunger in my stomach, so I take it. The fruit smells sort of like cantaloupe, so I tentatively lick the surface. The juice is sweet. I watch Tazhio scrape the inside out using his teeth, so I do the same. I've never been a fan of melon, but I'm hungry enough to eat a second and a third of these strange fruits when Tazhio shares with me.

"Let's wait to be sure your stomach is okay," he says, setting the basket aside.

I'm really glad he's here, because I would probably starve to death if I was stranded alone. I drink greedily from the jug of water, then lie back in the nest of leaves. "I bet my sisters are hungry," I say. "They don't know anything about surviving in the wilderness, let alone on an alien planet."

He stretches out next to me, pulling me close again. "There were a handful of crew on the shuttle. They'll try to gather the survivors and take care of them."

I remember the porter carrying Jennifer's case and pray he's with Jennifer and Suzanne now. He looked like he could protect them against giant centipedes and whatever else might be out there. I settle my cheek on Tazhio's chest so I can hear his heartbeat. "How long do you think it will take for a rescue team to find us?"

His body goes rigid for a moment, then he sighs. "I won't lie to you. We may never be rescued."

My breath catches and my fingers claw against his ribs. I've just had sex intending to get pregnant, and now I learn I probably have to give birth without a hospital, too? I try not to hyperventilate as I ask, "Why not?"

He explains that the planet's ionosphere not only blocks most scans; it creates a perpetual storm around the planet that's nearly impossible to navigate safely. "Even if they were to locate us and find a pilot willing to attempt a landing, there's no guarantee a rescue shuttle would make it down safely, let alone be able to take off again."

I feel numb. *I can never go home?* It's inconceivable. There has to be a way to get off this planet. I'm not ready to give up yet.

Tazhio sighs. "I'm sorry I let you down."

I frown. "What do you mean?"

"This was my first flight around the Singing Planet, and I knew it was dangerous. I shouldn't have allowed anyone to distract me."

I bite my lip. He'd been distracted, all right. Distracted by me. Then I tried to use Jennifer's app on my phone and everything went to shit. This is all my fault—well, mine and hers. "Don't blame yourself. I'm pretty sure my phone interfered with your controls."

He drums his fingers against my hip as if in thought. "I know it seemed to coincide, but the IDA vetted all human devices for safety compatibility."

"Maybe they didn't know about the changes my sister made to boost our signals."

"Well, whatever the cause, what's done is done. We have to make the most of our current circumstances. Once we're out of this, um, situation, we'll find the others and establish a camp.

What I've learned from the Sheeghr might actually be helpful."

I swallow. "Like the Gloor."

He nods. "Yes. And they can help us find food. The Sheeghr are friendly as long as they don't think a female is in danger."

"You think they really were trying to protect me?"

"Yes. But they may have trouble acknowledging our mating bond. In case you hadn't noticed, they're inherently promiscuous."

My back is still facing the main cavern, but I can vividly recall the sight of the frenetic orgy that accompanied our lovemaking. "But once I'm pregnant, they won't bother me, right?"

"I hope so, but I saw pregnant females in the orgy."

I shudder. "Thank you again for coming to my rescue."

He takes my face in both hands, looking deep into my eyes. "I'd die for you, Tamara."

"I hope it never comes to that." I try to laugh, but his words are too sincere to actually be funny.

TAMARA

$\mathcal{W}$e sleep again, and I wake to Tazhio nuzzling my neck. "I think we need to make sure there's a baby inside you."

I won't lie, his words sort of turn me on. I glance toward the cage bars, worried we might still have an audience, but this time not a single Sheeghr is even looking our way.

Tazhio's kisses turn to sucking and nipping, sending small jolts of pleasure through me. I lift a sleepy hand and run my fingers along the shell of his ear and down to his muscular shoulder, loving the solid heat of his body lying against me.

He lifts his face to mine, tongue caressing the seam of my lips, probing until I open to let him inside.

Little shivers of delight enter my bloodstream, and I let my fingers slide lower over his ribs. His heated skin is hard and smooth, and his weight on top of me is significant, but not crushing. It feels like a protective shield, and I tilt my chin up to kiss him back.

As his lips devour mine, I marvel at how gentle yet hungry he is. He tastes like sweet oranges on a hot summer day. Braced on one elbow, he cups the back of my head with one hand while the other slides beneath the hem of my blouse, leaving a trail of need across my skin.

His heated palm stops just below my breast, once more encountering my bra, but this time the clasp at the back comes undone as if by magic. I don't have time to ponder as his fingers slide underneath, massaging their way to my aching nipple. He rolls over the hardened tip with a thumb. I whimper, arching my chest up to meet him.

Using one knee, he nudges my legs apart, and heat floods my pussy. The hand at my breast travels downward to the waistband of my shorts. He pulls the drawstring slowly, making my breath hitch with every inch until the knot finally pops loose. Then his hand dips inside, the pads of his fingers sliding across my hipbone and toward my sex. He reaches the top hem of my panties—I'm so glad I wore my nice, lacy ones for this trip—and dips beneath the fabric with ease.

He finds the top of my slit and makes a deep, sexy sound into my mouth. Then his fingers glide over my mound, cupping my lower lips. One finger dips into my aching slickness, and it's as if a dam bursts. Heated moisture floods from me. I spread my legs and flex to meet him as he circles shallowly around my opening, pushing my lips aside and moving in wider and wider arcs until he's gliding over my clit, the sensation making me tense with anticipation and pleasure each time he rolls over it.

Slowly he focuses on the swollen bud, stroking up and down, dipping between my folds again and again. The pressure builds inside me, and my breaths match his pace, increasing in tempo until I'm panting with need.

As he strokes, he kisses behind my ear, nibbles my throat, his tongue hard, then soft, his teeth sometimes grazing my flesh as if about to bite. I grip his sides, bringing one knee up so I can pump against him in time to his rhythm on my clit. A frenzy is building inside me, a tightness that feels like it's borne of years of deprivation.

I begin to shake, my climax just out of reach. I need more. I need to be filled. Panting, I buck harder, encouraging his stroking to delve deeper, to penetrate me. But when he does, it's still not enough. I grab his wrist, panting. "I want you. Please."

Breathing hard, he pushes up onto his knees, exposing his cock to my view. Up close, it's bigger than I remember, shaped somewhat like a club with a pronounced head. A net of thick veins scrolls down its considerable length, visibly pulsing all the way to the base, where a small, sucker-like appendage sits right over his pubic bone. I vaguely realize that's what must've stimulated my clit while he fucked me senseless last time.

He grabs my shorts and panties and yanks them from my legs in one sure move. Planting himself between my thighs, he lowers his body on top of me. I feel his heat probe my entrance.

I keep my gaze on him, and his dark eyes meet mine with a look of satisfaction as he slowly pushes his girth inside me, millimeters at a time, stretching me with an exquisite pressure that makes my eyelids flutter. Wrapping my legs around his firm backside, I draw him against me until he's fully seated. My clit throbs as the bud above his shaft makes contact, and I swear it's sucking me gently, bringing me to the brink of orgasm. I let out a shuddering moan.

He lets out a breath, as if trying to maintain control. "You're so tight... so wet."

"Keep going." The pressure inside me is delightful, but I want him to move, to heat my channel with friction until I can't take anymore.

He pulls back, pausing. Just as I think he's about to pull all the way out, he slams forward again, burying himself until his hips crush against mine.

I gasp, mini-rockets of pleasure shooting down my legs to my toes. I thrust up to meet him. He takes up a steady rhythm, pumping in and out; huge, hot, throbbing. Every thick, hot slide feels amazing, nearly magical, as if he's melding with me, body and soul.

"So close," I pant. I'm right at the edge, but my body refuses to let go. My pending orgasm has built to such excruciating heights, I feel like it's going to kill me when it arrives.

I'm struck by the urge—the *need*—to take control. I want to ride him harder, faster. I want dirty and rough. I want to make us both come undone. "Let me," I beg, my words barely coherent.

But he understands. He rolls onto his back, taking me with him. Still locked together, I straddle him and sit up, pressing my palms against his gloriously muscled chest. He looks magnificent lying against the bed of leaves, his muscular arms reaching forward to grip my hips, his gaze intent on my face. "You're the most beautiful woman I've ever seen."

I don't feel beautiful so much as I feel fierce. Strong and unashamed. Fuck these aliens and their egg-laying monster. I've wanted Tazhio from the moment I saw him, and I'm going to enjoy having him, no matter the circumstances.

Tilting my hips, I rock down onto his hard cock. I've never felt so satisfied yet starving at the same time. I growl between my teeth, keeping my gaze locked with his.

He thrusts upward, gripping my hips almost hard enough to hurt, impaling me on his length. I shudder and clench, leaning back slightly for more friction and heat. His attention dances over my breasts, down my belly to our center of connection. I look down as well, watching him slide in and out of me as I ride him. The tiny appendage on his pubic bone can't reach my clit at this angle, but he circles my slick nub with his thumb. "Come for me, Tamara."

I'm so close, I can barely see straight, but I can't find the crest. I need more. "Please, Tazhio."

Something probes my ass again, entering me and adding to the fullness. My orgasm breaks into a monumental vortex of ecstasy. I cry out, my entire body quaking with release.

Tazhio's hands are like vises on my hips, and he groans, his voice matching my own. Heat fills me, geysering upward until I can feel it in my heart.

I whimper and collapse forward onto his chest, choking on my own labored breath. His chest is heaving, too, his heartbeat strong and fast under my cheek. Sweat slicks his skin and mine, while the musky scent of our union fills the air. I can barely keep my eyes open.

A gentle hand cups the back of my head, stroking my hair. "I love you, Tamara."

I sigh, feeling more content than I ever have before. "I love you, too, Tazhio."

TAMARA

The clatter of wood rouses me from my dreams. Tazhio's on his feet in an instant, and the sudden departure of his heat jars me to full wakefulness. I have no idea how long we slept, but my mouth feels cottony, and my nether regions are a bit sore. I suddenly realize I'm still naked from the waist down and search the leaves for my discarded shorts and panties.

Zeer is standing outside the cage, and one of the guards is removing slats from the enclosure. "Praise Gloor," says Zeer. "Fertility is complete."

I pull my clothes on, no longer caring if I'm discreet. The ferret aliens seem to have no concept of nakedness, anyway. "You mean we can go?" I ask, relief blossoming in my chest.

"Danger has been averted. No need to protect you any longer."

They really believed they were protecting me. I grab my bag and put it over my shoulder. Then another realization settles over me. "So, I'm pregnant? How do you know?"

Zeer raises her muzzle and inhales. "Obvious."

Tazhio takes my hand, a proud look on his face. My heart swells as I realize once again that he's mine for life and we're going to raise a family together. I just hope we won't be stuck on this planet, especially if I'll have to stay pregnant for the rest of my life.

"We thank you for your protection," Tazhio says to Zeer. "I hope this means our people can have beneficial ties with the Sheeghr in the future."

The Sheeghr leader nods briefly at him, but keeps most of her attention on me. "We are open to discussion."

I swallow, realizing that as a female-led community, they probably expect me to speak up. "Thank you for allowing me to choose my mate. Our ways are different, but I hope you can continue to respect that."

Zeer bares her teeth in what might be a smile and nods, fondling her erotically carved staff. "Respect is appreciated."

I'm not sure she really understood me, but right now I just want to get out of here and find my sisters and Beanie. As Tazhio and I walk down the terraces toward the cavern exit, the Sheeghr go about their business with hardly a second glance in our direction. Apparently, now that I'm pregnant, they have little to no interest in us.

When we reach the first terrace, Tazhio pauses to look out over the massive trunks and roiling roots beyond the cavern. Then he turns to me and grimaces. "I'm not thrilled with the idea of exposing the rest of the passengers to the Sheeghr, but I'm not entirely sure how to get back to the shuttle."

"Crap." I hadn't paid attention to our route, either. Plus, there was that carnivorous plant along the way, and who knew how many giant centipedes or other creatures? I swallow and glance around, relieved there are no pink penises in sight. "I wonder if they can draw us a map or something."

Just then, a three note ping comes from my bag. I jump. My phone? I thought I turned it off before we crashed. I dig in my bag and pull it out. A small red light is blinking in one corner. "What the heck?"

Tazhio looks over my shoulder. "What?"

"I don't know what this means." Other than the red light, the phone seems to be off. I turn it on. After a minute, the screen is active, and my mouth drops open. The app is still engaged, and there's a message from Jennifer. *Follow the arrow. Hurry.*

There's not a map, but a small green arrow points out toward the forest. When I turn the phone to show Tazhio, the arrow moves like a compass, always pointing in the same direction. "I think we can find my sister with this. Or at least her phone."

He takes my hand. "Then I guess you'd better lead the way."

Dear Reader,

Thanks for reading Tazhio and Tamara's story. We'll be seeing them again in the next book featuring Jennifer and her hunky blue porter, Nazhin. More drama, more laughs, and a lot more steamy action as they try to come up with a way to escape the Singing Planet. Tap the cover below to preorder your copy, or keep reading for a sneak peek...

As the owner of Demod Industries and one of the Intergalactic Dating Agency's top sponsors, why am I pretending to be a lowly ship's porter?

Until next time!
Love, Tamsin

NAZHIN

SNEAK PEEK

NAZHIN

I take another sip of *Lensoran* bubbly, letting the sour fizz linger on my tongue as I watch the blue-green planet called Earth grow larger in the viewport. Two cabin stewards—both blue Kirenai like myself and also in human form—bustle between the shuttle's empty rows of plush red seats, readying everything for the first human passengers. Earth is the most exotic destination in the galaxy at the moment, off limits to unauthorized surface traffic, and I'm the only "guest" currently on board, having pulled a lot of strings to get on this flight.

I'm curious to meet my first human, but that's not why I'm here. My marketing team needs images and sensor data to promo our new line of sensors, and this is a great chance to get rare footage of the strange new planet.

One of the stewards pauses next to my seat. "We're almost ready to land, sir. Can I get you anything else?"

I hand him my glass. "No, thank you."

We'll only be on the ground long enough to pick up our human guests—all female—for the IDA cruise, and I need to double check the atmospheric sensor mounted on the outside of the shuttle before we take off again. The IDA charged me nearly as much for the permits to install my equipment as I'd paid in bribes to get a seat on the shuttle, and the trip will be a waste if the sensor isn't working.

The moment we touch down, I stride toward the hatch and wait patiently while the boarding ramp unfurls. Hot, humid air sweeps in, making me nostalgic for my home on Kirenai Prime, though here it smells of bitter petrochemicals rather than sweet happa fronds. I pause at the bottom of the ramp to take in my surroundings.

Our shuttle is the only vessel on a pad made of some sort of hard-packed aggregate painted with white and yellow lines. A strip of shorn green foliage runs down one side of the landing pad, and crude buildings sit in rows in the distance. I can make out tiny figures moving around near the structures, but none show any sign of approaching us.

While the stewards position themselves next to the ramp to await guests, I move to the nose of the shuttle and double check the settings on my company's sensor. Everything is within expected parameters, so I upload the data already gathered before stepping away to take a few promo shots for marketing. The view near the vessel is less than spectacular, but I didn't coordinate any extra time for exploration. I activate my comm chip to capture images of a few of the buildings. Perhaps the marketing team can use the "study primitive cultures" angle to sell a few of our products.

A grating rumble reaches me from the other side of the shuttle, so I move around to see a long, boxy vehicle coming to a stop. A female with red-gold hair climbs out, and I start recording as she engages a steward to take her luggage. He leads her up the ramp, and I swivel my recorder back toward the vehicle.

Three other females are getting out, and a human male is removing luggage from the rear of the vehicle. A female with dark hair struggles to remove an enormous case from the rear passenger door. Her sleeveless blouse and shorts expose pale skin that intrigues me, and I wonder if it's as soft as it looks. My own current human form is based solely on holo images provided by the IDA to help Kirenai guests look appealing to the human females.

After a moment of recording, I realize she can't budge the box on her own and rush forward to help. "Please allow me to assist."

My *Iki'i* immediately registers warm tendrils of gratitude as she turns to me. "Oh, God, thank you. I almost dropped it."

Her hazel eyes connect with mine, and I suck in a breath. She's the loveliest being I've ever encountered. Her brown hair glints with auburn highlights and is held away from her face by a silver clasp decorated with pointed stars. An intoxicating smell surrounds her, like the petals of a *malila* flower. I stand there holding one end of the box until she raises her eyebrows. "Do you need another porter to help you?"

Porter? I flush with embarrassment, realizing the other end of the case still rests on the seat inside the vehicle. I pull the case easily from the vehicle, determined to prove I can easily lift anything she needs, even though I'm not part of the crew.

"Please be very careful," she says. "This is expensive equipment."

The case is more awkward than heavy as I hold it against my front and follow her toward the shuttle. I can't help letting my gaze slide down her back to her pert ass and bare legs. "What sort of equipment, may I ask?"

"Astronomy. I'm writing a thesis on the atmospheric properties of an exoplanet we'll be passing during the cruise."

Beautiful and smart. I'd been on matchmaking cruises before and never found a mate—finding a genuine match is rare for Kirenai. But I'm already obsessed with this female, despite having known her a matter of moments.

We reach the top of the ramp and I wave off the steward who tries to take over. "I've got this."

Inside the shuttle, she turns toward me. "Where can I stow this?"

I blink, then cut a gaze across the cabin. "I'm not sure."

The steward gestures toward the back. "If you would follow me, sir, I can show you."

Her mouth drops open. "I'm so sorry. Are you not part of the crew?"

I should tell her I'm not, but I want to keep helping her. So instead, I smile and say, "I'm here to serve. My name's Nazhin."

"Jennifer," she says, following close behind as I carry the case to where the steward indicates.

My mind is spinning with all the questions I want to ask her, and my crotch is aching with other needs. I haven't felt so strongly attracted to anyone in ages. After stowing the case, I turn around to find her holding out what looks like a slip of colored paper.

"What is this?" I ask, taking it between two fingers.

"A tip." She frowns. "But I guess Earth money probably doesn't do you much good, huh?"

I chuckle and hand it back. "A tip isn't necessary. Though I'd love it if you'd sit with me for the flight up to the *Romantasy*."

Wariness pings my Iki'i as she takes a half-step backward. "Sorry, no. I realize this is a singles cruise, but I'm only here for my research. Thank you, though." Without even a glance back, she turns and sits next to a woman with copper-bright hair.

My *Iki'i* reels as if it just collided with a wall. I don't think anyone has ever dismissed me like that, and my chest aches with an uncontrollable desire to be near her. *Should I tell her that my company specializes in high-end sensor design?* Certainly she'd be interested in that. Then again, she was very clear that she's not interested in being social.

I settle into a seat a few rows behind her, unable to take my eyes off the back of her seat as I ponder my options. She's not even open to getting to know me. How can I pursue her if she won't let me near her? And the longer I look at her, the more the need to be near her her grows.

She's here to do research. I glance toward where her case is stowed. I bet she'll need to lug her equipment around, and will ask for a porter. All I need to do is to be present whenever she needs a hand. And if she thinks I'm part of the crew, well...

The difficulty will be in keeping the secret long enough for her to get to know me without ever actually lying. And the more I ponder it, the more I like the idea. Smiling to myself, I lean back in my seat. I've always enjoyed a challenge.

JENNIFER

My sister, Tamara, and I step off the lift to discover a maze of fancy velvet ropes winding across the shuttle bay floor between us and the purple rosebud shaped shuttle. I've spent three days dodging alien advances and enduring tedious soirees awaiting this excursion through the ionosphere of exoplanet RAx-P-7—known as the Singing Planet to the rest of the galaxy. I've seen hazy images of it taken back on Earth, and I'm giddy with excitement over the opportunity to document the atmospheric spectrography up close.

Traveling to space has been my dream since Dad gave me a junior telescope for my eighth birthday. The first moment I viewed the night sky through the eyepiece, I knew I wanted to be an astronomer. But after my lab partner ex-boyfriend stole a year's worth of research and published it as his own, I thought my dream might be lost for good.

Until my twin sister, Tamara, won tickets for this alien space cruise. Now I have one last chance at a Hail Mary to turn in my college thesis on time. So, while most of the other women on board are here for the hot aliens, I'm only interested in viewing the stars and testing my new app. Nobody on Earth has ever had a chance to capture telemetry like this before, and I know I'm going to blow my professors away with this thesis.

Ahead of us on the shuttle deck stands a small gray alien in a white crew uniform who looks like he came straight from Area 51. He's talking to a pair of tall, broad-shouldered Kirenai wearing Speedos.

Tamara nudges me with her elbow and tosses her chin toward the Speedo-wearing guys as they thank him and enter the empty maze. "Jennifer, look."

I chuckle. "Nice."

Somehow, the aliens got it into their heads that human males wear swimming trunks on cruise ships. Now almost every alien guest we encounter wears them—and not only when they're at the pool. Not that the eye candy is a bad thing—I never imagined aliens could be so good looking, from the blue Kirenai shapeshifters to the gargoyle-like Khargals. Even the short red aliens called Fogarians aren't terrible to look at if you can get past their red body hair and beards.

"More Bloom sisters! How delightful," the gray alien says. The crew is really good about remembering names, and have bent over backward trying to make us comfortable.

The alien at the podium points a thin finger toward the shuttle. "Your other party member is already here. Please have an enjoyable trip!"

"Thank you." I lift the nearest rope and duck underneath it. I want to get to the shuttle and set up my equipment before the good seats are all taken.

Tamara grabs my arm and hisses, "They have those here for a reason, you know."

I scowl at her. Sometimes I wonder how she and I can be twins when she's such a scaredy cat, but I adore her anyway. I gesture to the empty maze. "It's not like I'm cutting in front of people."

She clutches her big purse closer, one hand inside it to pet her emotional support dog, Beanie. Our other sisters were opposed to her bringing the animal, but I know Beanie is the only way Tamara can face stress, so I don't mind.

After a brief moment of hesitation, she grimaces and ducks under the rope with me.

I give her a proud wink and hurry forward, ducking and winding until I spot our sister, Suzanne, skulking near the shuttle ramp. A pastel swirl scarf is wrapped around her head and neck, and sunglasses hide the rest of her face. She's been trying to avoid a Kirenai admirer she hooked up with on the first night of the cruise.

But my sister and her shenanigans aren't what draw my attention. Next to her waits Nazhin, the tall blue porter I met the first day of the cruise. He's carried my equipment a few times since then, and each time I see him he looks a little different. He's completely ditched the Ken-doll haircut so many of the other Kirenai have and is now completely bald. He's also developed outlandishly huge muscles—I assume because he's been hauling stuff all over the ship. Even here, from across the shuttle bay, I can see his biceps straining the short sleeves of his uniform. *I wonder what he looks like in a Speedo...*

I hope you enjoyed this sneak peek of the next story in the Kirenai Fated Mates series. Will Nazhin's plan to get closer to Jennifer work? Is Jennifer going to be able to gather the data she needs? And most important, will she ever get to see Nazhin in a Speedo? ;)

NAZHIN will be hitting Bookstores on October 3, so be sure you don't miss it and preorder your copy now!

PREORDER NAZHIN

GLOSSARY

Bacca - a game that resembles frisbee golf

Burendo - a Kirenai who excels at shapeshifting and is able to not only assume the form of other species, but coloration as well.

Fogarian - aliens with red hair and sideburns who live on a rocky, mountainous planet.

G'nax - a species that uses light to communicate attraction and arousal. They also have a symbiotic relationship with an eight-legged insectoid.

Hage - bald, wide-eyed alien that looks much like the iconic alien humans have circulated.

Happa trees - blue fronds resembling palms.

Hypawa - species with magma colored eyes.

ICC - Integrated Circuit Chip - an embedded chip that is an alien version of a holographic smart phone

Ijin'en - four legged herd animal raised for meat and well known for its stupidity.

Iki'i - empathic power.

Irn - a unit of measure. One planetary rotation around the Kirenai's sun.

Jiro - a unit of measure equivalent to approximately two Earth hours.

K'ogai - the town near the palace on Kirenai Prime.

Kazhitu - nuts that look like sticky buns when baked. High in sugar, buttery and fruity.

Khargals - gray horned aliens with stone-like skin and wings from the planet Duras ;)

Khensei - a toxin that causes Kirenai to denature into their resting state.

Kikajiru - my distracting one - a term of endearment.

Kirenai Prime - the Kirenai home planet. Purple and blue with swirling white clouds.

Kuzara - shit, damn, fuck.

Kryillian death swarm - tiny insectoid creatures that can kill a man within seconds by sucking his blood.

Lensoran bubbly - alien champagne

Lonala moth - fragile insect native to Hypawa

Malila flowers - fragrant, night-blooming flowers popular in conservatories across the galaxy

Matrix/cellular matrix - the term for a Kirenai's cellular mass.

Nilgawood - a tree used to make resin.

Oritsu - An expression of awe.

Popotan - the plant used to line ship interiors that provides oxygen, recycles water, is highly resistant to radiation, and can regenerate itself if damaged.

Qalqan - a species known for their healers. Good bedside manners due to their resistance to emotional fluctuation.

Resting state - a Kirenai's amorphous shape, like nakedness to humans, it is shown only to family or trusted friends.

Senburu - a galactic conglomeration of merchants who oppose the emperor's rule. Individual members are called *Senbur*.

Sireta Prime - a popular party planet.

Sowain - tastes like chicken!

Supo cloth - smart fabric for clothing that doesn't need buttons or zippers.

Teozhisa - a cart to carry people.

Tolonovone - a device that creates lighted markings

on the skin. Used by G'naxians as part of their mating rituals.

Ukimi ice - beloved dessert with cool, spicy flavor like sweet mint.

Urru - purple egg-sized fruits from the Singing Planet that taste like cantaloupe

Vatosangans - species with alabaster skin and blue or green hair who tend to be stocky or rounded. Planet is called Vatosang.

KIRENAI FACT SHEET

Kirenai are an all-male species of shapeshifters with a natural form (resting state) like an amoeba who usually assume a bipedal shape to interact with other species. Until the discovery of humans, Kirenai required a permanent pair-bond with a female of another species to produce offspring. All Kirenai traits are dominant and located on the Y chromosome; male offspring are fully Kirenai, while female offspring are fully of the mother's species.

Birth rates have been historically low, and over the ages, the population has dwindled. Human females are exceptionally receptive to impregnation, and do not require formation of a pair-bond to conceive, which has made Earth a target for black market slave traders who deal in "breeders." The Emperor is making attempts to protect the population.

Regardless of the shape a Kirenai's matrix is in, he cannot change his skin or hair color. The most common color is blue, although hues range anywhere from mint green to lavender. Rare individuals, called *burendo*, can vary coloration outside this range. Kirenai blood is clear or slightly milky unless infected, when it grows murky to almost solid white.

All Kirenai have empathic abilities called *Iki'i* which make them capable of reading emotion and desire, and also enables them to identify individuals within their own species regardless of shape. This is the only Kirenai trait sometimes passed on to female progeny. The ability also makes the species consummate lovers because they can take actions and form attributes their partner finds most appealing. Bonded mates assume a permanent form pleasing to their mates; rarely can they force themselves into an alternate shape after bonding.

The average Kirenai life-span is approximately eight hundred human years. When a pair-bond is formed, a Kirenai passes a small genetic market to his mate that mitigates the aging process, giving the mate a lifespan to match his own.

OTHER GALACTIC RACES

Qalqan – A pink, lizard-like race who are innately skilled at medicine. They have more than two genders and change genders as they age, which makes reproduction rather complex. It also means means they rarely pair-bond with Kirenai. In addition, their emotions are hard to understand for others and unreadable by Kirenai *iki'i*.

Hypawa – A race with large, expressive eyes, smooth luminescent skin, and luscious hair on their heads and eyelashes; considered by many to be the most beautiful race in the galaxy. Their origin is a mystery - even their supposed world of origin doesn't seem to be their homeworld. Their economy is dependent on tourism and entertainment.

G'nax – A spiny, bug-like race that can breathe a variety of atmospheres. Biologically they are inclined to be traders and have senses that let them navigate through hyperspace. They use light to communicate attraction and arousal. The females have a symbiotic relationship with an eight-legged insectoid which secretes dew used to feed G'naxian infants.

Khargal – A horned, gray-skinned race that can enter a hybernating state where their body becomes stonelike. The number of horns indicates the amount of royal blood in them. Honor is more important to them than anything. They have wings and claws and resemble gargoyles of Earth mythology. Their planet of origin is a barren world that has two moons and is known for having some unusual ore deposits and relatively few life forms.

Fogarian – A burly, thick-skinned race with crimson hair, claws, and fangs. They come from a high-gravity planet rich in crystalline gemstones and excel at digging. The females usually bear litters of two to four offspring, and are favored mates for Kirenai. Fogarians tend to be very straightforward and keep their promises, even if it means death.

Vatosangan – A small, slight race with alabaster skin, rounded features, and blue to black hair. As the most common race to pair-bond with Kirenai, some say they actually control the galactic empire behind the scenes. They seek any alliance, technology, or advantage that will benefit them, and their current government is a meritocracy.

Klen – A green-skinned humanoid race with eyes on extendable stalks. Their tongues can act as prehensile limbs, and they have the ability to withstand a wide range of temperatures. They are a race of scavengers and can modify some of their bodily secretions to become various useful substances.

Hage – Short, bald, gray-skinned aliens with large heads. They were the first to make contact with humans. Though their scrawny frame doesn't suggest it, they are addicted to the pleasures of taking nutrition, and their cuisine is spectacular. A past war obliterated their homeworld, and they now live scattered among the other races, usually employed in a service capacity.

Sheeghr – Not advanced enough to be admitted to the Galactic Confederation. A matriarchal, ferret-like race native to the Singing Planet. Known for hypersexuality, the females maintain a constant state of pregnancy to ward off a native parasite called a Gloor. Any female who refuses or who cannot get pregnant is killed. The males determine rank based on the size and color of their phalluses.

Human – New members the Galactic Confederation. This bipedal race has not yet homogenized into a single language, culture or appearance. The species has skin tones that vary between black and alabaster, with shades of brown in between. The females are capable of reproducing with many other species throughout the galaxy, and have become a target for illegal slave trading.

INTERGALACTIC DATING AGENCY

Looking for more out of this world romance? Your local Intergalactic Dating Agency can help! These strong, smart, sexy aliens are on the prowl for mates, and humans like you are exactly what they're after. Jump in with Book 1 of any standalone trilogy from our crew of rock star SFR authors and make steamy first contact! Warning: abductions may or may not be included!

Grab more hunky alien action here:

http://romancingthealien.com

ALSO BY TAMSIN LEY

Midnight Heat

Wild Child

Kirenai Fated Mates (Intergalactic Dating Agency)

Arazhi

Zhiruto

Iroth

****POST-APOCALYPTIC SCIENCE FICTION
WRITTEN AS TAM LINSEY****

Botanicaust

The Reaping Room

Doomseeds

Amarantox

ABOUT THE AUTHOR

Once upon a time I thought I wanted to be a biomedical engineer, but experimenting on lab rats doesn't always lead to happy endings. Now I blend my nerdy infatuation of science with character-driven romance and guaranteed happily-ever-afters. My monsters always find their mates, with feisty heroines, tortured heroes, and all the steamy trouble they can handle. I promise my stories will never leave you hanging (although you may still crave more!)

When I'm not writing, I'll be in the garden or the kitchen, exploring Alaska with my husband, or preparing for the zombie apocalypse. I also love wine and hard apple cider, my noisy chickens, and attempting to crochet.

Interested in more about me? Join my VIP Club and get free books, notices, and other cool stuff!

www.tamsinley.com

bookbub.com/authors/tamsin-ley
goodreads.com/TamsinLey
facebook.com/TamsinLey
instagram.com/tamsinley
tiktok.com/@tamsinley?
amazon.com/author/tamsin